The Kind
of Things
Saints Do

The

John

Simmons

Short

Fiction

Award

University of

Iowa Press

Iowa City

Laura Valeri

The Kind of Things Saints Do

University of Iowa Press, Iowa City 52242

Printed in the United States of America

http://www.uiowa.edu/uiowapress

Printed on acid-free paper

The publication of this book was generously supported by the
University of Iowa Foundation and the National Endowment
for the Arts.

Library of Congress Cataloging-in-Publication Data

Valeri, Laura.

The kind of things saints do / Laura Valeri.

p. cm.—(The John Simmons short fiction award)

Contents: The kind of things saints do—Whatever he did, he
did enough—She's anonymous—A rafter in Miami Beach—
That easy kind of life—Hugo, Arthur, and Bobby Joe—Turn
these stones into bread.

ISBN 0-87745-819-7 (pbk.)

1. United States—Social life and customs—20th century—
Fiction. I. Title. II. Series.

PS3622.A45K56 2002

813'.6—dc21 2002018058

02 03 04 05 06 P 5 4 3 2 1

To my family

Contents

ACKNOWLEDGMENTS

My deepest gratitude goes to all the faculty and
administration at the Iowa Writers' Workshop
and the Graduate College at the University
of Iowa for the opportunities they have given
me and for their invaluable guidance, without
which this project could never have happened.
I also wish to thank everyone at the program
in creative writing at Florida International
University for the unflagging support that
enabled me to forge ahead in spite of doubts
and difficulties.
I must also acknowledge my indefatigable
readers—Rebecca, Brandt, George, Jay,
and William—for their good advice on
my manuscript and for their friendship.
Finally, I owe a special debt of gratitude to Paul
for his trust in me and for inspiration.
Thank you all, and bless you.

The Kind
of Things
Saints Do

The Kind
of Things
Saints Do

For the last five minutes Chip's been going on
and on about how we can still be friends, blah, blah, blah, blah. So
I blow smoke right at his face, and I tell him to shut the hell up.
He stares at me like he's all hurt, like he's the one who's getting
dumped, and he combs his hair back with his fingers and says,
What are you being so hostile about? I get out of his blue Dodge
pickup truck and slam the door real hard and as I walk up the
steps to my house I shout, You come here again, my dad'll whup

your ass real good. And he shouts back, Yeah? Dare him to try it, something or other but the screen door slams shut behind me and anyway what do I care what he says? He's gone.

Dad is slouched on the couch, still up and drinking, smoking his stinky cigars, a cloud of his smoke drifting around his chin. He says, Susan, that you? Where the hell've ya been, missy? His voice is reedy and high-pitched like he's been getting high on some kid's balloon at the Firemen's Carnival. From the trail of crushed beer cans that I'm kicking as I walk in, I can tell he's wasted. I hear Dad's slurred voice starting on his usual song and dance: You no good this, you no good that, when you gonna get a job or what? And I can tell from the way he's chewing on his smoke, holding it in the inside of his cheek, shifting his jaw just before he lets it out, that he's ready to beat on something and better fun if that something will put up a good fight. So he blinks at me through a tuft of that smoke he's been gurgling with, and he says, Susan, didn't I tell ya not to hang out with that moron no more? Where ya goin'? I'm talking to ya.

I gotta make it past him through the living room to make it safe to my bedroom, so when I see him trying to get up from the couch, the springs squeaking like a hiccup, I sprint under him and beat him to the move, slamming one in his fat belly, my fist like going through foam. I leap just past him, squeezing between the couch and the TV, and I make it in time to shut the door on that ugly moon face of his, locking it just as he says, Come outta there. Come out and lemme teach you a lesson.

I take off my jacket with Metallica's *Reload* that I painted on it myself—my masterpiece yet!—and I put on my Van Halen album loud enough to make my teeth vibrate. Who cares? Maybe a neighbor will get pissed off enough to call the cops, let Dad sober it out in jail. But I never get that lucky. If cops weren't so goddamned lazy Ma wouldn't be ashes in a box someplace upstate. And if social workers had eyes I wouldn't be stuck in this goddamned cave with Dad guarding the mouth, either, those bastards.

Dad's shouting he's gonna knock down the door if I don't open up. I lie in bed, flipping through *Rolling Stone* like I got all the time in the world. Anyway I have to figure out what the hell to tell Lisa and Dana tomorrow about Chip dumping me for good. I never even liked the kid all that much, but in this lousy town you ain't got a chance in the world if you ain't got no boyfriend.

Don't get me wrong. I don't care that much what kids at school think of me, but hey, Lisa and Dana are my friends, right? Not like I get to pick and choose, with Dad being the sub from hell giving me the rep at school. Sometimes a girl needs a place to crash at when Dad's so drunk he's dangerous, and fuck it if it's Lisa's or Dana's, 'cause the cops sure wouldn't do nothing for you if you begged them. Ask Ma. If all you got is a dad who was born with the whiskey bottle in one hand and the other bunched up in a fist ready to strike at anything that moves, and a Ma who was staggering and stupid all the time, too weak to do nothing but weep till the day she drank herself to hell, you need your girls to come through for you. So I got me Lisa and Dana.

OK. Lisa, I don't care so much about. She's just this dumb chick with big boobs, thinking that guys are all there is. But Dana, she's all right. Dana's my girl. We're always together we twos. I look after her from the kids at school. She needs me. Her parents don't know kids. They have these statues in the yard, St. Anthony, St. Francis, St. Catherine of Siena. They think the saints are going to take care of everything or something. They even have some weirdo guy, this Padre Pio. They got his picture right up in this hallway that they call a *vestibule*, like some kind of grand entrance thing. I look at the picture every time I crash at Dana's. Seems kind of creepy, this bearded old guy looking down at you from this circle of light, his hands all bloody. Dana says it's called a stigmata. Supposed to mean you are a martyr saint or something, that bleeding thing. I tell her it's creepy, all the blood coming out from those holes in his hands like he got stuck climbing up a spiked fence. Dana says it's the pain of other people's sin that makes him bleed. She says Padre Pio asked to suffer and God gave him the stigmata so he could be like Christ. I shake my head and say, Shit, Dana, that's just creepy church-freak stuff.

Meanwhile here I am, with Dad slamming his big fat body against the door. I'm looking at the magazine and I see this picture of this chick who's got her arms all tattooed up with these cool, forked-tailed dragons with jagged mouths belching out a spray of blooming orchids. And just then I remember this girl I saw once at the park in front of my house. She showed me how to carve names on your arm with a knife. It was like this big fuck you, to show that she could take the pain, nobody could really hurt her. So I'm thinking maybe that's what Padre Pio means with his big holes: Look at me bleeding, all you assholes out there.

Then I start thinking of how saintly little Dana would freak out over all those cuts, so I do it. I take out my knife from my boot, the one that Chip gave me for my birthday, and I roll up my sleeve and I go at it. Slow. Starting from my wrist up so it reads backward like some radical satanic message you get on those vinyls from the sixties and seventies. I'm real careful too. I go at it letter by letter so you can really read what it says, not like the chick at the park where it was all just one scratchy blur. The cutting gets a little messy at one point, the blood spilling down my arm, my wrist, like I'm trying to hurt myself for real, but I wipe all the blood off with my T-shirt and already I can read the PI.

Sweet.

Outside I can hear Dad saying something about getting me tomorrow, but hell, tomorrow he's gonna be so hung over he won't even remember he has a daughter. I raise the volume on the stereo and I'm blasting Van Halen so loud I can't hear myself think. My arm's shaking, and blue, and all those cuts bleeding like crazy while David Lee Roth is letting out those high-pitched screams that make my toes curl. I see all the blood soaking up in my T-shirt and I hear the lead guitar whine and moan and them shouting *The cradle will rock* so I bite my lips and go at it again with the knife, even though my eyes are so full of tears I can barely see, even though I can't stop my arm from shaking and hurting, even though I feel like screaming my head off myself.

———————

So I missed homeroom again. And Mrs. Dobson, the dorkhead principal, is sitting there going like I'm setting a bad example, my dad being a substitute teacher and all. So, yeah, yeah, I act like I'm all sorry and I just shake my head, keep a low profile, 'cause dork-head here doesn't like it when I look her in the eye. Thinks it's some kind of challenge. I've already got a couple of suspensions this month so I have to play her game. A few more months and I'm outta here, I'm gone. But if dork-head here decides to screw me, I have to stick around one more year or drop out without graduating, and it's like Dana says, you can't even pump gas without a high school diploma.

When I'm out, I'll get a good job, so I can get a place for Dana to come live with me. I could have a family for once, take care of Dana like I used to take care of Ma, and screw Dad. Let him get drunk and kill himself with booze if that's what he feels like doing. Lately, when Dad gets in my face, his muscles bunching up and his fists ready to slam 'cause his dinner ain't salty enough or his left sock feels tighter than his right, I just get this feeling like one day I'll put my knife right to his balls. I wanna get out before I do something bad. But first I have to get through this—school, Mrs. Dobson, all that.

I tell myself, Bite the bullet, Susan. Just give her what she wants. So I nod and I say, I'm sorry, Ma'am. I have to, you know, look at her real softlike with my eyes full of tears. Dork-head thinks I'm about to cry the way her voice suddenly goes soft. Figures. Hell, I need a cigarette so bad I'm sweating, but I got my eyes on this little book of passes hanging at the edge of her desk, so I tell her I'm getting real hot, and I take off my jacket. And wham! I put my arm slam on her desk, face up so it's right under her nose. My jacket, I drop on top of the passbook where dork-head ain't looking. Even though she shuffles her feet under that chair looking off to the side at this fake plastic fig plant she got I know she can *feel* the masterpiece on my arm, all black and blue around the scratches. She can feel it on her eyeballs, I know it. But dork-head snorts in her hands like nothing. She speaks into her collar when she says, Well, now try to be punctual next time, young lady. *Punctual. Young lady.* I nod and I pick up my jacket and the passbook and leave her sitting on her fascist ass.

So much for counselors up my back all day. At this school you could kill yourself. They'd just kick you to the side until the garbage truck shows up.

I head for the bridge off at the edges of the courtyard. That's where you go to smoke cigarettes or a joint if you got one. It's a tough crowd out here. No honor student or virgins. I'm a virgin, but shit, you wouldn't know it by looking at me.

When I tell Dana I'm out here, she gets this look in her eye like she's watching me get felt up by some motorcycle gang. She won't admit it, but Dana likes this shit, the bridge, the knife, and all that. She likes that I have the guts to beat up somebody for my turf. Dana never had the face to walk right up here and park her ass here on these concrete blocks they got standing for railings and take out a cigarette and smoke with an air like, Got something to say about it?

Yeah, you got it. Dana's that wimp every kid with some bug up her ass wants to beat up on, the kid that'll make you feel good about what a loser you are. Dana's got no attitude. She's got her weird-shit church parents and all her high grades and all those freak-oh sweaters that make people shit, like this one she has with the face of a little girl with red hearts on her cheeks. The braids on the little girl are these strands of yellow wool braided up in big chunks and stuck on top like somebody stitched them on as an afterthought. And the braids stick up from Dana's chest when she wears the sweater, and you look at that and you don't know if you should laugh 'cause she looks like she's twelve or get hot because of the braids sticking up from her big boobs.

Kids around here don't get Dana, so they do shit to her. They yell stuff at her. She gets weepy and scared, and that makes them feel like they got something on her. Me, they don't like me neither, but they don't mess with me 'cause I got a knife and I could mess them up if I wanted to. So I start to feel sorry for Dana and I hang out with her awhile. She's like a puppy, following me around all the time. She comes over to my house and sees Dad hollering, tools hanging from his two-size too-loose pants, drunk, even right after school, and Ma shrunk to a picture in my underwear drawer and a pile of ashes in some box upstate and she goes Susan, oh Susan, how you suffer. Susan the suffering makes you strong. With her mom and dad driving her around to violin lessons, and voice lessons, and French lessons, and then home by seven, dinner by eight, at nine homework and TV, ten go to sleep, and never ever talk about a date or a movie, so Dana, well she's like living in cartoonland or something. I kind of wonder what she thinks she knows about suffering or about being strong. But then she gets this real sweet face, her lips puckering up. She hugs me all warm and soft and says, Oh Susan, you poor thing. I smell her, the way she's been sweating a little, this vanilla soap she uses, and sometimes it's like I'm with Ma. I'm hugging Ma.

So it's all right. I can forgive Dana a lot of shit. But now she's got this thing for Lisa, always hanging around her like Lisa knows everything there's to know. It's Lisa this, Lisa that, like I don't exist no more. Shit, I don't need nobody or anything. But sometimes it gets me kind of pissed off to see them twos arm in arm, whispering stuff, breaking out laughing like only they know what's funny. I gotta get me back some respect.

So I'm sitting here at the bridge, and I see Gene Pereira coming up the hill, this kid Lisa and Dana think is so hot. I light up a cigarette and see him strolling up here and I think maybe this could be my lucky day. Lisa's crazy about the kid. She would shit if she knew I got it going with Gene.

Gene's got that usual dumb grin on his face as he comes up to the bridge, a hop to his walk like he's got springs in the heel of his ratty old sneakers. And he's singing. With his arms open, hugging air, head tilted up like he's waiting for God to piss on him.

He sees me and says, Yo, Sue, you know I got the lead in *South Pacific?*

I say, Shit, dude. You gonna tell me again?

Last week he got the lead and now he thinks he's something, like he's too good for the bridge now, even though he can't keep his skinny white ass away from here. Gene scratches his crotch real loud till he sees me looking at him. So then he looks around and pretends like he's got bitten by something, scratching his thigh and his calf.

Fucking mosquitoes, he mumbles.

It's January, mind you.

Gene's just a loser with an attitude, like me. He hangs out at the bridge most times shooting the crap from the side of his mouth, failing out of every class, filling up the filing cabinets of every social worker in America with his arrest record. Then he gets lucky at a try-out for the school musical and it goes to his head, like he got something to give to the kids around here. Like he made it out of the ghetto and he's coming back to save us. For weeks he goes wearing a jacket and tie to school saying we all have to have respect for education. He says he's going to make it to Harvard, just have to apply and keep the faith. Now the latest thing with him is the faith, Jesus saving you and yeah, yeah, all that jazz, like he's been hanging around Dana one day too many. The jacket and tie, that was last week. I figure the faith thing will last another week or two, just 'cause it annoys most of us so damn much.

Right now Gene's got that fat silly grin spreading on his face like grease on a skillet, and I smile at him from the side of my mouth as I take a drag, trying to see why Lisa thinks he's all that. I waltz up to him and he stands right in front of me, silly grin and all, singing with his arms open *Some enchanted evening.* Then he says, Good morrow. Yeah, really.

I laugh and call him a loser. He gets all billowy, filling up with air, his neck sinking into his shoulders like he's mad, but I know what he wants is everyone looking at him. Dana and Lisa melt every time Gene's around, and Lisa, that loud mouth, she goes showing off her megatits to Gene every chance she gets, wearing tops that she cuts up herself with the scissors so her big boobs hang out even more, but he acts like he don't care. When Gene's around she points at the cover of the stupid magazines she reads and says, One day this is going to be me. And Dana loves it. Dana says, Lisa's so funny. She's so crazy! She's so wild!

Gene says, Foul language makes us sound like we're not smart enough.

I roll up my jean jacket so my scars show nice and wiggly, with the word PIHC bright brown against my pale, pale skin. Maybe that'll shut him up about that *foul language* stuff.

I say, Hey Gene, did you know that God makes the saints bleed?

Gene looks down at my scars and says, That's new. He sticks his cigarette up the side of his mouth and rolls up his sleeves to show me his biceps, which I must admit are nice and hard, with little dips and curves. Gene shows me a tattoo, a heart with a snake coiled around the arrow that breaks it splat in two, and initials that I can barely read, but something like DF, I think. Gene says, This is art. He nods at my arm, rolling down his sleeves, satisfied like a pig in shit and says, That's mutilation.

Mutilation. The kid'll do that to you, come up with some word you'd figure Mrs. Dobson stapled to his detention slip or something. But I know he ain't as stupid as he looks, so I say, Why would I be so dumb to scar myself with that cheesy sentimental shit.

Gene just laughs. He laughs, oh, ho, ho, ho. Takes the cigarette from the side of his mouth and lets out a little curl of smoke, then oh, ho, ho. And then, *Some enchanted evening . . .* This girl sitting near these bushes over where the bridge ends looks up this way and says, Shut up you guys.

I go, So Gene, you still working AV?

Gene barely stops to eye me and catch his breath; then he's off again, singing. So I take another drag and I hang there with my cigarette between my teeth, looking at this big, moss-coated stone near my boot, thinking how I'd like to make him eat it if he don't stop singing. Gene belches the song right at my face, his hands crossed on his heart like he's serenading me or something, and the chick by the bushes with these colored dream-catcher earrings sticking to her neck is looking all pissed off. She says, Shut up already.

I'm afraid Gene is going to turn around and give her some smart-ass answer that's going to get her going so I get right to the point and I go, Hey, I got the key to the spot room. Wanna go do something?

Gene stops singing. The spot room's where all that electrical stuff is stored, and only Dad, who's been working AV on the side, has the key this year. With Dad being a substitute and all, they think they can trust him. It's a fucking joke. Dad has been selling spare parts from the AV school equipment pretty much since he first got the job. No one works spotlight except when a show is on, so the spot room is like this great hangout to go smoke a joint or make out. It's the best-kept secret in school; Dad'll only let you up there if you grease his hand good.

But I don't go off feeling good about Gene smiling at me quiet, because he's got his eye on something back by the bushes, where the girl with the dream-catchers and some other skinny girls in ripped jeans and fringed leather are passing around a pipe. Gene waltzes over to the chick with the dream-catchers and asks to bum a cigarette. I mean, a cigarette! He says, Nice earrings, his fingers touching the tiny feathers on the dream-catcher. The chick says, Get lost, and she turns around like he ain't even there. So Gene lights up, takes a few puffs, and comes back over, bouncing and slapping his arms around his chest, complaining about the cold.

I say, Gene, this ain't California, you know? I don't know what planet you're on, but the rest of us are still stuck here in Rye, New York.

Gene looks back over at the dream-catcher chick and says, No kidding.

I don't even know if he's talking to me. Then he goes, starting to hum again. Shit, like I need this. Suddenly he says, What's up with your dad?

He ain't here today, I say.

Gene nods, smiling kind of crooked. And it takes me awhile to figure out that he's thinking about the spot room. By now I kind of pushed it in the back of my head, Gene being the smart-ass that he is, letting all that time go by, like he never even heard me say it.

I say, Don't worry 'bout my dad. He ain't sober enough for subbing today.

Gene gives me this long look, and for a minute here I'm thinking it might not be all that hopeless.

So I tell him, That's why I got the key. Supposed to turn it in to Mrs. Dobson.

And that's when Gene says, Well, I can meet you up there in about fifteen minutes or so. He looks over his shoulder like he don't want the dream-catcher chick to hear, which pisses me off. What am I? Consolation prize or something? But I only got another few hours before I meet up with Lisa and Dana in the cafeteria, and I got to have something to brag about to make up for Chip, get some juice back, some respect from my girls. So I spit out my cigarette and I snuff it with the heel of my boot and I say, Don't keep me waiting or I might change my mind.

Just to give him something to think about.

Gene doesn't say shit. In fact, it's like he never even heard me. He's waving at this other kid, Bubba. Bubba sees me and says, Tell your boyfriend! Tell that ugly mother fucker he owes me twenty bucks.

So I have to get going 'cause that kid hates me and I sure as hell don't want to spread it all over school that Chip dumped me, and when I'm far enough where Bubba can't get at me, I say, Tell him your fucking self, Bubba. I ain't your goddamned mouthpiece. Bubba starts yelling something at me, all I hear is Bitch something or other, but I don't care. I got a date with Gene Pereira in fifteen minutes, and I ain't got a clue how I'm going to deal with it. Like I said, I'm a virgin. And it's not like it's going to be easy explaining *that* to Gene.

So once I ask Dana, What makes a saint a saint. She thinks about it for a while, fingering her chin, touching her forehead with two fingers like it's a fortune cookie and it might crack if you want to read what's inside. Then she says, It's faith.

Faith?

And she goes, Yeah. Faith. Hope. Belief. They believe so hard they make things happen.

And then they're saints?

And then they're saints, she says.

So what kind of things can a saint do when she's a saint?

Things, Dana says, slapping her hands on her thighs, like the answer is so obvious even the flies get it. She says, Like miracles and such. Like making water into wine or curing people who are sick.

So for a while I start hoping for Ma, like if I believe it hard enough I can make her rise from the ashes or something. But then I think maybe Ma coming back is just too big to think about, her being in a tin box and all; maybe I should think about something easier, like me and Dana busting out of this town, getting a place of our own, living together like sisters. I think about it so hard it gives me a headache.

Then Gene shows up. I hear him fumbling with the door down at the bottom of the stairs. I've already smoked half a pack of cigarettes. I figured I missed European history and if I show up for geometry now, Mr. Hall, pencil-prick, is going to mark me absent anyway, just to prove a point.

I can hear Gene stumble up the stairway, and I freeze up. All the curses I want to chuck at him the moment he walks in are one big block in my stomach, and I get a cramp right under my belly. So I light up another cigarette and throw a leg up this beat-up old couch that's older than the Bible. Gene stumbles in. He says, Hi. Says nothing about the fact he's had me miss two classes already.

But he stands there, slapping his hands together, swinging his arms back and forth, and I'm thinking maybe he's nervous. So I blow smoke at his face and I say, Gene, you're a loser.

I get up and I grab my purse, hoping he'll stop me. I mean, lunch is just half an hour away. But I gotta make some sort of scene here for the way I've been hanging out waiting. It smells so bad from all the smoke and the sweat, I don't want Gene to think I'm part of the stink. But I grab my backpack real slow, slipping my arm through it, kick at some coiled-up cables.

Gene says, You leaving?

At this point I'm expecting him to be like he usually is, not caring what I do anyhow. I kind of want him to start singing so I don't have to feel like I have to do something to make things cool. So I look at him as I snub out my cigarette on the wall, leaving a nice long black smear. Gene's reading what I want in my face or something, 'cause he goes, Gimme a cigarette.

I say, Buy your own.

He says, OK, but gimme one.

So I give him one, and he says, Gimme a light.

I say, Screw you, but I dig in my pocket for my lighter.

Gene sticks the cigarette in his mouth and nods at me, like I should bring the lighter to him or something. I strike and say, Give me a break, and he cups his hands around the flame and sticks his face out so the cigarette can take. Then his hands drop to touch my wrist. His mouth is pulling at the cigarette, his eyes squinting from all the smoke curls, but he looks straight at me. I guess he's not a bad-looking kid. I guess he's Lisa's type. Tall, muscled, and tough looking, his eyes serious and squinty like he's staring into a spotlight. He's not my type. Even Chip wasn't my type. I don't even know what my type is, but I guess it don't matter. Guys to me all look like Dad: drunken slobs waiting to pound on me for some reason or other. What matters is to get respect, get that badge to wear out on my sleeve for Lisa to know I'm the thing. No one's going to get the better of me.

But when Gene looks me in the eye, his hand around my wrist, I get a funny feeling in my stomach. It ain't from his touching me, either. It's just that all of a sudden I'm picturing Dana up here, standing in my spot, holding a lighter, and getting her hands touched, and I feel my belly go soft and funny. It's kind of creepy how she popped into my head when I'm thinking of what Gene's going to do with me.

Gene pulls me to him and I don't say a word. I even let him slide his hand up my shirt, let his fingers slip under my bra. I'm thinking, What's wrong with me? All I'm thinking about is Dana. I close my eyes. Gene puts his mouth over mine. He stinks sharp with menthol and ash, but I don't mind now because it's not my mouth he's kissing. I'm seeing Dana's mouth in my head, those puffy soft red lips getting kissed by a mouth, not even Gene's mouth, just some anonymous mouth. In my head I see a hand fumbling up Dana's sweater, the stupid one with the girl with the braids, and I get all excited like I never got with Chip, even when we both smoked pot and made out for hours. I keep seeing sweet little Dana with the kinky hair all wrapped up in a bun, with the round breasts and her chubby stomach. Dana, yes, Dana. Gene touches my stomach and I picture a hand on Dana's stomach. It gives me a shock to imagine her shirt being pulled up. I throw my head back and I gasp like this big burst of feel-good wants to come out of me all at once. I feel for Gene's hand and I move it down to that spot between my legs that's aching now. He breathes hard and goes crazy biting my neck, Dana's neck. He grabs at my crotch really hard like he wants to crush me but I'm light inside, 'cause I'm thinking Dana. Oh wow, Dana.

By the time Lisa and Dana get to the cafeteria I've already been sitting there fifteen minutes, sucking on an empty can of soda, shifting on my bony ass for the burning between my legs. I see those twos before they see me. I think about waving them down, but nah, I catch myself before I look like a dork. They'll see me. I look down at the biology book, forging dork-head's signature on a pass from the book I stole, excusing my absence from first, second, and third period. I don't want everyone to see me mooning at those two like a loser. But I look up real cool when I hear them.

They're standing nearby, holding a tray of macaroni with meat. I think they've seen me, but they just sort of hang out together, talking hushed, like they got some secret they gotta pass like gas before they get here. The smell of the glue they call food around here is making me sick to my stomach.

I'm still all shaky from Gene. What we did up there is sinking in all of a sudden, too fast for me to make out if I'm happy or pissed. I look at Dana giggling, Lisa getting close to her, talking in her neck, her big mouth moving close to Dana's perfect little ear, with that little stud diamond earring I can see glowing even from here, and I get a picture of her up there in the spot room, Dana, moaning and tongue kissing. Suddenly I feel like someone just punched me in the stomach. 'Cause it's like it was Dana I made out with up there in the spot room. I think of that real flashlike, and it's like I just touched a wet socket or something, and before I can stop myself I'm going, Dana! Lisa! Over here! Waving them down like I want to stop myself from thinking.

This chick next to me, she looks at me real funny. I want to tell her something that'll make her turn around, but a feeling like touching a live wire's still going through me. I get these thoughts cluttering up in my head. I want to crush the soda can and bounce it on the forehead of this dumb chick who's staring at me. I want to get out of here. I want to go over to where Dana is and . . . I don't know. I don't know what's what. I look at Dana out there with Lisa, and I get a feeling like when I used to see Dad getting his hands on Ma, getting his wet mouth all over her face. I get a feeling like I want to rip him up from the earth like a bad weed.

I wave. Lisa—I know she heard me. She turns around and gives me this sideways look. She knows I don't like her, Lisa, and she don't like me neither. Nobody says nothing, though. That's the deal. We share and keep quiet. Except I tell Dana that Lisa's just a big slut, and Lisa tells Dana that I'm a loser. But we don't say it obvious like that. We laugh about it. *Ha, ha, Lisa is such a slut.* We just pretend we're all one big happy family. And I'm all the more happy to have this thing to rub in her face about me getting it on with Gene. I'm thinking how I'm going to bring it up so I can stick her face right into it, so she can smell the stink of her own jealousy.

Finally they come over, like Excuse me, we take our time. Dana, she looks down like she knows she's not doing right, but she can't help it anyhow. I'm thinking how I'm going to wipe off that smug smile from Lisa's dumb face. First thing I do is take off my jacket like it's cool and fiddle with the pass so it's not obvious I'm showing off.

Sure enough Dana shrieks, My God! What happened to your arm?

For a few seconds I do like I don't even hear her. Then I look up real cool and I go, What?

Dana goes, Your arm! What happened?

I look down and I go, Oh yeah, that. Chip. He got on my last nerve. We're over.

Lisa rolls her eyes. She goes, Oh, *please.* You're such a loser, Susan. Some guy goes off dumping you and you go cut yourself up like that.

Dana squeaks, Susan, how could you do that to yourself!

Lisa says, Chip's not going to feel it, you know?

Dana says, Oh my God, Susan, you should go to the nurse. I mean that's dangerous stuff. You could get an infection. You could get hurt! That must hurt.

Dana repeats herself like I don't get it. And she's freaking out, her hands rubbing her cheeks real hard, her teeth biting her lips. She goes, My God, is that going to get infected? What if you lose your arm or something? And Lisa is like, Oh *please.* She's *not* going to lose her arm. Oh *pleeease*, she just did it to show off. She did it so Chip would feel bad for dumping her.

I didn't say Chip dumped me.

Lisa looks down at her macaroni, smiling, stabbing her plastic fork so hard it bends when it hits the bottom of the plate.

I say, I just spent all of third period fooling around with Gene Pereira.

Dana says, What? She says it like soda went down the wrong pipe.

Lisa doesn't say shit. She just looks down at her macaroni. She grabs a big forkful and stuffs it in her mouth, her lips all greasy, her cheeks bloating up. She looks at me with her eyes slanted like she could stab me with her look.

Dana says, You did what?

But I'm looking at Lisa. This thing is between us twos, really. Something about her getting into Dana's head that I want to make her pay for. So I say, I just lost my virginity with him. Fifteen minutes ago.

Lisa says, Bullshit. She laughs a little, like, ha ha, how cute. She says, Come on. You're kidding us, right?

I lean back in my chair, cross my arms, and say nothing.

Finally Lisa says, How? She makes that sound like there's no way in hell that could have happened. I can tell she believes me. She knows. Something's telling her and it's eating her up.

I say, I just asked him, and he said yeah. Then we went up to the spot room. I got the keys from my dad this morning.

I take out the keys and dangle them right in front of Lisa's nose.

Lisa's mouth hangs open a little. With all that tit flaunting she had going, it probably never occurred to her to just walk up to the guy and ask him to fuck her.

Lisa clasps her hands around the edges of her chair, she pushes forward, her stomach pressed against the table, and she says *Bullshit!* Her voice comes out from the back of her throat and it's like she's hissing, a vein bulging on her temple, something on her neck pulsing like Dad's neck pulses when he's about to hit. I'm almost laughing. But I try hard to hold it all in, because laughing might make her think I'm lying.

Go ask him, I say.

Lisa's face is getting this dark shade of pink. Her lips are pressed together like she wants to spit at me. But she won't. Lisa is nuts, but she ain't stupid. So she just squeezes the edges of the chair till her knuckles get white, trying to look like it's nothing. She turns to Dana and says, Well I told you that guy wasn't worth it.

All the time I was so busy looking at Lisa, I didn't even look at Dana. Her face is bright as if she's been jogging, and her eyes are all shiny and wet. She's shaking her head, looking at me. She says, Oh Susan . . .

I get this feeling like something tickling the inside of my chest when I look at her, but I ignore it, and I tell her, Now you're the only virgin left.

Dana just shakes her head. She says, But Gene . . . me and Gene . . . And then she bursts into tears all of a sudden, just like that. And I mean real hard sobs. I'm thinking, what's going on here? I'm watching Dana's chest bounce up and down with the tears and I can't figure it out. I'm feeling bad, suddenly, for doing Gene. I feel all dirty inside. I wanna reach over to Dana and ask her what's wrong, but all these kids in the cafeteria are looking at her cry. These girls at the other table roll their eyes, and giggle and I just want to shove their ugly faces in their stinky lunch.

I shout, What're you all looking at?

They keep giggling but they turn away. I turn around just in time to see Lisa put her arm around Dana's shoulder. I get this feeling like someone just started me with jumper cables. Dana drops her head on top of Lisa's chest and sobs. She says something about a phone number or something, she says, He gave me his phone number, but I don't get it. Dana and Gene?

I tell her, Dana, I don't care about Gene. You can have Gene if you want to. Lisa gives me this vicious look, but she's got her hands touching Dana's head like Dana is her pet. I'm all dizzy from seeing Lisa's hand on Dana's hair. It's like I can feel Dana's hair through my fingers; it's like I can feel Dana crying on my chest.

Lisa yells, Don't you get it? She doesn't want Gene anymore, now that you slept with him. You've ruined it for her.

I know I should say something nasty to that bitch. I know I got something in me to say that would make her shut up once and for all, but it's like all the bad-ass stuff was just blown out of me or something, and all I want to do is make Dana feel better. I want to touch Dana, put my arms around her like Lisa is doing, make her feel good and make her need me like she needs Lisa, want me like she wants Gene. And then I think, something's wrong with me for thinking this. But Dana's crying and it don't matter.

I tell her, Dana, I'm sorry. I'm so sorry. I didn't know. I thought . . .

But suddenly it's like, hard for me to talk. Because I realize that I want more than anything in the world to be sitting where Lisa is sitting and to hold Dana in my arms, to feel her sobbing on my chest. I get this feeling down between my legs and I feel something warm turning in my belly. But at the same time it's like my chest is made of glass on the inside and someone went around smashing things with a baseball bat. I don't know why I feel so bad, like when I used to hold Ma after Dad slammed the door and left her crying with her elbows on the kitchen table and her hands holding up her hair. Except it's not quite the same. I don't know what I should say to Dana. Maybe if I could just touch her . . .

Lisa yells, Get out of here Susan. Get out.

The Kind of Things Saints Do

The kids in the cafeteria, I can feel them looking at me, I can hear some of them making this violin sound, like it's all some soap opera, some corny little show. I just keep looking at Dana, like maybe she'll say something, that it's okay and that she don't care what I did and we're still friends. If she could only say something then maybe I wouldn't feel like such a circus freak. I wait for her to talk to me, standing there on my feet saying, Dana? Dana? But she don't say nothing. She just sobs on Lisa's chest, and Lisa pets her head and says, Oh, don't take it so bad. Oh, they're just not worth it. And when Lisa looks up at me, she says, Get out of here Susan. You're making her cry.

For a moment I want to rip Lisa's hair from her head. I want to punch something. I want to hurt somebody. And I think I can understand Dad, the need to crush something you want that you can't hang on to, something that hurts you so bad. But I hear Dana sobbing and it's some pain that goes from the top of my skull down to the sole of my feet. I realize I gotta get out, 'cause I ain't got nothing to do but get out.

I kick at a chair. Fuck Lisa and Gene and Chip. And fuck Dana. Fuck everybody. I even leave my jacket and my book of passes right there on the table. I gotta get out, push all this out of my head, Dana, Lisa, everybody. So I'm a freak. Hey, I can take it. There's space for the freaks too, ain't there? Like that saint garden at Dana's house, like that Padre Pio, bleeding his heart out from his hands in a shrine, like it done anybody any good, his bleeding.

I walk out the back door to the yard and head for the bridge. I got my cigarette already between my teeth and I'm smoking, sucking on my cancer stick like it's a goddamned oxygen tube and I'm under a ton of water. The chick with the dream-catcher earrings is there. She sees me, she goes, Hey, you got a cigarette? I throw the damned pack at her so hard it bounces off her chest. But she goes, Thanks.

I go at my boots and I take out the knife.

The dream-catcher chick says, What're you doing? I sit down next to her on top of the concrete block on the bridge, feeling my hands shake, feeling that need to hurt something. I look at her and she looks at me with half a smile. She brings the cigarette to her lips. I'm still looking at her and she giggles. I study my left arm for a minute, then my right. I take the knife in my left hand,

and I get started on my right arm, first one line, then another, careful, so the skin won't bleed too much. As the skin tears this pain shoots right up to my brain. It's so sharp and sudden everything else is numbed.

The girl with the dream-catcher earrings says, Sweet.

I rub my eyes dry from tears so I can look at the letter D on my arm, and I go, Yeah. And I get started on the A.

Whatever He Did,
He Did Enough

For many years he would remember the first time he knew he was in love: Clara leaning with her arm on the doorpost, a sleeveless white dress tight around her bronze skin, her feet bare against the Spanish-tiled floor. Her hair is cropped short above her delicate ears, her face is childlike and elfish. Stan is on the bed. He yawns and devours her image with his stretching mouth. She is thumb-size, standing in the doorway: a fey spirit leaning against the lintel, a pixie queen in the light. She has just come out of a bath, and her wet breasts draw round shadows on her dress where her nipples strain against the fabric. He inhales her with the *cafe negro* brewing in the kitchen. She is chicory and soap.

"¿No quieres desayuno?" she asks.

It's almost noon. They're in Cuba, in her mother's house, where he met her, where he rents a room for a few dollars every night. She is offering him breakfast. Her front teeth look uneven as she smiles, and he notices then that her mouth is too large on her face, that it blooms, generous and calm, on her chin. He runs the back of his hand against his chest and laughs. When she jumps on the bed on top of him the springs groan and the legs squeak against the tile. He feels her weight on him and a yielding inside, strangely pleasant. Dream girl. "Chica de mis sueños," he says. His voice comes out hoarsely. She takes his words on her tongue, her mouth hungry on his mouth, on his nipples, on every finger of his hands. She is smooth against his skin, her bones fitting snugly within the hollows and curves of his limbs. He runs his hand over her short wet hair. The mouth blooms on her face, swells up on her sharp cheeks.

She whispers, "Miami, ¿tu casa?"

"Yes, I'll take you with me," he answers her question between kisses: a small, complacent lie she must have heard before from other men.

Over the years he will recall when she held her arms to him, pushing six hundred dollars in the palm of his hands, even as his head shook no.

"Tengo dinero," she said, breath short. "Te pago." She had money. She would pay.

The banknotes spread in her hands like a fan. She fell to her knees, her hands clasped together over her bosom. "Necesito salir de este infierno," she said. She needed to get out of this hell. He looked at the money fan and thought about her in the nightclubs where he'd seen her, dressed up too expensively for the money he knew she didn't have. Once in awhile she'd disappear with a man hooked to her gaunt arms. Once in awhile she returned from somewhere dark, her dress rumpled, her eyes glazed and a little cold. She said she was a dancer.

It didn't matter. Looking down at the weeping Madonna grimace on her pretty face, it didn't matter what she said she was.

"I can't," he tried to say, but he couldn't speak. She was on her knees. She held on to his hands, her great mouth puckered with the whispering of a strange prayer.

"Miami. Tu casa."

He nodded at her elfin face and bent down to kiss her mouth, kiss her mouth again, and drink her ripeness, her newness, *cafe negro, chica cubana,* girl of his dreams.

———————

Edgar had both hands on the small of his back and tilted his pelvis, waiting for Stan to answer. Stan didn't make eye contact. He gave Edgar no warning or explanations about Clara moving into the house they shared in Miami Beach, but most things Stan did, he did differently from most people. That, he figured, explained it enough.

"Twelve goddamned fucking rolls of toilet paper in four days," Edgar said. "What does she do with it, your *cubanita*. Is she fucking supplying the whole fucking black market in Havana?"

Stan didn't like the way Edgar kept calling Clara *your cubanita,* but he couldn't think of anything worth saying. Edgar paced around the living room with his hands clasped behind his head, looking at the hammock Clara hung from the ceiling earlier, weighed down with tropical plants, yellow and white flowers exploding under a thick tangle of dark leaves.

"What is this?" Edgar asked, hand raking through his hair. "What-is-*this*? My God. Hello? Hello?" He snapped his fingers in the air, his wrist flapping back and forth. "This is South Beach, dear, not the Tropical Gardens. I *refuse* to live with *this*, OK?"

Clara sat on the couch with half a grin on her mouth. She said, "Dios mío, qué maricón!" He acts so gay! Stan pretended not to hear her.

Then Edgar followed Clara to the kitchen. Stan heard them fighting from the living room. He had to type out his plasma supply survey of the Caribbean area for a trade magazine that had already paid him for the work, so he tuned out the argument, eyes focused on the scratchy notes he took on his trip. Once in awhile he was distracted by Clara's awkward imitations of Edgar.

"Banana and vanilla taste *redun-don*. It's no taste interesting," he heard her say.

Edgar, after that: "Redundant. The word is redundant. And I said *doesn't. Doooe-sn't.*"

After some time, Stan heard a thunk rising out of their strained voices and something dry and small skittering on the floor, a shower of small beads of a sort.

"You fucking bitch! . . . Someone call a fucking ambulance. Goddamn . . . I'll sue you. I swear, I'll sue."

When Stan walked into the kitchen he thought only of the money he hadn't saved. Edgar held his head with both hands, a huge lump forming where Clara hit him on the right side of the head, a spray of blood staining his white fingers. But Stan saw more clearly the lentils: hanging from Edgar's curls, clinging to his cotton shirt, floating in small pools of water on the floor, stuck in the cracks between the tiles, fallen on the metal plates over the burners. Stained-blood lentils like watered-down gravel covering the whole of the kitchen floor.

Clara sighed, rolling her eyes. "¡Qué dramático!"

She was still clutching the pan.

Magda, one of Stan's ex-girlfriends, referred them to a friend for a sublet in South Beach. "It's not the pretty side of South Beach," she said on the phone, "but it's the Beach nonetheless."

With Clara unemployed, himself on a tight budget and still paying Edgar's medical bills, Stan took it. The apartment building was a run-down low-rise next to an abandoned elementary school and a coin laundry walled with rusted machines crawling with spiders and palmetto bugs. The police sirens woke him up at night, their cars jetting through the narrow streets, rubber peeling and screeching on asphalt.

Magda stopped by sometime after they moved in to bring them *arroz con pollo*.

"I cooked the dish myself with real saffron twigs and free-range chicken," she explained.

When she stepped through the door she clung tightly to Stan, kissing him on the cheek and calling him sweetie, oh sweetheart, and dear. She was wearing a perfume he vaguely remembered tasting once, on her neck and between her thighs. She pecked him on the mouth, holding on to his face. "Coochie, you look warn out." Her hands felt warm and slightly damp on his cheeks.

Clara glanced up but remained seated in the living room, even as Stan waved her to him. Magda gave the Tupperware with the *arroz con pollo* to Stan, breezed past him through the vestibule, and waded through the stacks of opened boxes still full of books and clothing, finding her way to the living room and Clara.

"Cuando tú quieras ése saborcito cubano," she told Clara, "te vienes a mi casa, ¿me oyes?"

Stan watched Clara's glance slide from Magda's black silk blouse to her heavily heeled designer shoes and felt that same glance like an itch on his skin. Clara turned back silently to the television set.

Magda repeated the invitation to Stan: "You guys are welcome any time. Any time, you hear? Whenever you crave that Cuban taste."

"I like to live in America," Clara chanted, forcing her accent. Stan understood the intended insult for Magda, who was Cuban but born in the United States.

"Venga," he reprimanded Clara. Come on now.

Clara spread and rearranged her body over the length of the love seat. The tips of her bony brown knees sprouted momentarily above the backrest, looking like the joints of a giant locust. Her sandaled feet pushed into the armrest.

Stan glanced down at the *arroz con pollo*, sliding his hands around the cover of the Tupperware container. He knew, of course, that Clara had a hard time with Cuban Americans. *They politicize everything*, she said. But they aren't patriots who left the island with their leather suitcases and their fancy clothes, abandoning *hermanos* to the struggle in the thick of the trouble. When they met her, she said, they wanted her to say that Havana was a sewer and that Castro was the Antichrist, but what did they know, these Cubans who were weaned on American cheeseburgers and diet Coke? Like she owed anybody anything for where she was now.

Stan couldn't think of the right words to explain, so he just smiled with the side of his mouth at Magda and shrugged. Magda smiled back. Just as wide. Her mouth seemed somehow connected to his through the space and air between them.

"Doesn't Clara want to meet me?" Magda asked Stan.

Clara peeled herself from the love seat. Her sandals clacked lazily against the tiled floor. She clacked past Magda and Stan toward the kitchen, where she opened the refrigerator door and, after a moment of indecision, chose a pint of pistachio ice cream. She spooned out a few dollops, savoring the cream on her tongue, letting it all disappear into her pouty mouth but for the shaft of the spoon. Then she set the spoon-speared tub on the kitchen table, padded to the bedroom, her sandals clacking and clacking, and finally shut the door on them both.

Stan watched the creases Clara made on their bed with her weight. In the candlelight she looked surreal, an undulating canvas of moving lights and shades. He remembered something of her, the way he saw her one night dancing on the beach in Cuba, dancing for Chango, for safe passage to the Americas, her head bent backward, her hands twisting and bending with the wind, her moving feet kicking the sand with frenzied steps. She was something to him then, something he could not describe. He had felt her inside him, pressing against his ribs, draping around his veins and arteries like an ivy made of the essence of a soul. What happened to that girl? He looked at her in the swaying candlelight, remembering shadows on her moon-bathed skin, shadows projected on her by the branches of sand pines wrestling with the wind. Was she still that blooming ivy or just a strangler fig?

"I don't have any more money than that," he said to her.

"Then why you go drink?"

Her English was better but not good enough for the restaurant job Stan had arranged for her. She had been fired today, and then she went looking for another job at a strip club. Stan dug into the pocket of his jeans draped over the chair next to the bed. He found his wallet and pulled out another twenty-dollar bill. He only had a five left. He reached for his shirt on the floor and pulled it over his head.

"Hey." Clara held him by the arm. "Why you go drink without me?"

Stan pulled his arm free. He walked out of the bedroom without a word. On his way out the door he caught a glimpse of her turning flat on her belly, her body stretching naked over the sheets. She remained naked like that in his head as he walked out, right on that bed, her perfect buttocks dappled by the flickering candlelight. He thought about the man who saw those buttocks. Did the man ask her anything when she stepped on the stage for her interview? *What is your name, honey? Another fucking rafter. Can you speak ass? Can you speak pelvic thrust?* Stan straddled the motorcycle, stepped on the kick start, his body precipitating like his mood. He could see it in his head: laughter, raucous and sprayed with the scent of whiskey. He'd known plenty of men like that. He'd seen plenty of places like that, too.

"Is all I can do here," Clara had said. "You crazy? I no sleep with this men. Just dance. You say I must go work. So? ¿Oyes?"

The road lights stretched in front of him, turning into a strip of artificial flambeaux. There she was inside him, ivy girl, tightening around his veins, his muscles and tendons, tightening up, tightening. *You fool. You stupid fool. She only wants to help.* Her ass, up on that stage, lifting, dropping, swinging from side to side in front of a man's face. What did she wear? A strap of green underwear swallowed up by her muscular buttocks.

You fool. She just wants to help.

His friends were all there at the same bar, standing by the pool table, playing darts, watching the basketball game on TV. Their greetings blasted through the smoky spaces as he walked in.

"Stan! There he is! Broke out of jail, huh?"

He strode up to the bar and set the helmet right up on the counter. He slid his hand into his back pocket for his wallet and made eye contact with a woman. She smiled at him through the opaque mirror behind the bar. He recognized her but didn't know her name. His hand was still in his back pocket when someone's fingers wrapped around his wrist.

"Honey, let me do that." And then a female hand was in his back pocket, sliding up and down over his buttock. It was Magda.

She always knew when to find him, how to make him feel good when he needed it. Stan held her wrist, slid her hand out of his pocket, and reclaimed his wallet from her fingers. The bartender set a mug of pale ale before him. Stan spread the five open on the counter, his last bill. He looked into the mirror again, hoping to find the other woman.

Magda talked into his neck, close to his ear. "Where have you been, dear. That girl keeping you all locked up? How selfish of her."

He thought, How much money can a girl make swinging her ass in a bar? More than five dollars. More than twenty. He slipped his hand between Magda's thighs, his fingers searching her damp warmth.

"Well, that's a hint," she joked, but she didn't stop him. He glanced again in the mirror for the woman who made eye contact with him earlier, but he couldn't see her.

He caught a glimpse of her later, taking her drink to a table farther back in the bar near the jukebox. He made a mental note of it as he stepped down from the stool with Magda hooked to his arm. He tasted Magda's mouth once before he took her back to the alley to her car. She had been drinking gin and tonic. Her tongue was cold and spicy. He ate her mouth with kisses, but he wanted something else. In the car he gently led her head down to the zipper of his jeans. She took the hint and rubbed her hands up and down his bulge. He closed his eyes, his fingers tangled in her hair, then slipping under her sweater, reaching for her breasts.

Keep the thing going. He twisted her nipples between his fingers. Magda was gentle on his penis, slow. Her mouth was patient on him. His hands forgot her momentarily when the pleasure scurried up his belly, through his throat, down his legs to his toes. *Keep the thing going.* He grabbed the back of her hair. *Keep the thing going.* And there she was, Clara, dancing on the stage again, her ass dappled with candlelight. A man's hand pinched those dapples. A man's finger probed between her buttocks, pulling at the green strap of her bikini. Stan saw the hair on the man's finger and Clara's head thrown back, her neck arching under a flashing strobe, her mouth moaning. *Keep the thing going.*

He pulled at Magda's hair. He pulled her up to his face.

"You fucking bitch," he said, kissing the cum on her lips.

Outside the car he remembered to ask about her kids.

She told him they were with her ex tonight and slipped both hands in his pocket, escorting him like that back to the bar. He gave her one more kiss just before they stepped in, his hand tangled in her hair behind her head, pushing her face to his. Inside, a friend patted him on the back, asked him about stats on a basketball game. Stan searched the darkness for the nameless woman he saw in the mirror earlier. He saw her talking to a very tall, very thin man, a celery stalk of a man. He said to his friend he didn't know about the game, hadn't been following.

"Jesus, Stan." A scowl, and then, "Clara got a job yet?"

Stan shook his head no, and in a breath asked for a loan for drinks, for the woman whose face was familiar but whose name he didn't know. For dignity he stepped up to the jukebox, flipped through the CD selections, jingling coins in his pocket as though he'd make a choice.

Someone said, "Clara? With a mouth like that, I'd bet she'd make a fortune giving head."

It was an accident. He knew he was not supposed to have heard that. The comment came from a voice soaked with drunkenness. Some of the guys huddled around the one who spoke and changed the subject, talking loudly about the game, cursing about the score, the unfairness of the referee. Some idiot had the bad sense to laugh. Or maybe Stan just imagined it. He didn't lift his gaze from the jukebox. He thought it would be a mistake. It would make him have to face the insult, say something about it, and answering to the insult would be obliquely admitting that there might have been a truth to it. The bartender raised the volume on the television. The Knicks had scored again against the Heat.

Someone yelled, Fuck! Fuck! Fuck! Fuck! Fuck!

He could get into a fight tonight, and that would be fine. He was not drunk enough, but better. But then it was too late. No one was paying attention anymore. He turned away from the jukebox. His friends were shouting, jeering, and Clara, Clara was standing on the bar counter, wearing spiked heels and a shiny green tongue bikini. Her long legs strode the length of the bar, and myriad hands reached up to her, reached up and pinched her nipples, fingered her belly button, grabbed handfuls of her thighs. She wasn't here, Clara. She wasn't here, of course, but she could have been. It all could have been true.

The nameless woman slipped from the booth she'd been sitting in, her purse clutched to her breasts. She made eye contact and said, "Hi. Remember me?"

He said, "Of course."

She slipped something into his hand. A paper napkin. The tall skinny man came out of the bathroom before Stan could ask her anything. He said to the woman, "You ready?" And the woman followed the celery stalk man out of the bar. Stan looked at the napkin. She had scribbled her phone number on it in brown lipstick but not her name. He put it in his shirt pocket and pulled out the fifty his friend had loaned him. He planned to spend it on drinks for himself and for Magda. He would get to fuck again just before he left here, and that would make it three times he got it tonight. Once with Clara. *That fucking bitch.* The burning in his stomach made him noxious.

Hours later he stumbled to the parking lot, Magda unwilling to wean herself from his arm.

"I gotta go," he said. "Gotta go. Gotta go."

"Call me." She kissed him. Her saliva on his lips stunk, made his stomach turn. "Who's that bitch you got at home, anyway?"

"I gotta go." He straddled the motorcycle and slipped his helmet on. Magda watched him, her legs spread apart, her fists on her hips. He kick started and revved the motor. Her skirt flew up as he pulled out of the parking lot.

Magda yelled, "She ain't better than me, you asshole."

Clara said that every day he stayed out longer. She said his meetings with his clients became ever more frequent, his business trips longer. She said, Stay home. She said, Don't go drinking without me anymore. Stan ate his dinner, stared at the television without speaking. Clara cleared up the plates. She ran them under the faucet and placed them in the dishwasher, and Stan went to the living room to watch the eleven o'clock news. He watched that and then watched the late movie. When he went to the bathroom he found Clara hunkered on the floor, a tipped box of laundry detergent at her feet, her hands grasping the powder and tossing it up like wedding rice. Her face looked distorted, a caricature of rage clinging to her forehead and cheeks as though she'd painted it on with makeup.

"¿Porqué no te casas conmigo?" Her voice pushed harshly through her lungs, bouncing almost physically against his face. Why don't you marry me, she said.

He reached in his pocket for his pack of cigarettes, stalling for an answer. Then he said, "You don't like it like it is, go somewhere else." His ears were burning. He wasn't sure if he had meant it.

She said she couldn't bear to be a nothing. *Una nadie. Una cualquiera.* It was disgraceful to live like that, she said. She followed him into the living room, her voice a clapping in his ears. He sat in front of the television set, turned the volume up high.

She asked, "¿Y esto?" What is this? She held a paper napkin to his face. He squinted to see it against the television glare, but she rubbed the napkin hard on his mouth. "¡Cerdo! ¡Cerdo!" She screamed. She called him a pig, shouting at his face.

The napkin glided to the floor, and Stan saw the phone number, the lipstick.

"So what!" He shouted. "Yeah. So what!"

He became aware of his own panting, of the blood rushing up to his forehead. For as long as he could remember they'd been around, women, stalking him like cats from darkened alleys, dancing like shadows around his steps, or unwinding slowly around his hands, his waist, his neck, like smoke rings. There were women on his business trips, women in restaurants where he dined, women in the bars where he drank, women who walked up to him without saying a word, their phone numbers scribbled on napkins that they pressed into his hands, women who wrapped their bare arms around him and danced with him hip to hip, leaving scented gossamers of their perfumes on the skin of his neck.

"So what? So what?" He shouted at Clara so hard that her eyes squinted. He felt a longing for those women. Where were they? Where had they disappeared? He used to love his life the way it was. What happened? What happened to him? To that man who hitchhiked to Nairobi and Cairo, that man who used to jump out of airplanes in his spare time, that man who rafted through the Costa Rican forest on the river Pacuare. He felt his heart pumping in his chest as he shouted, "So what? So fucking what? I always come here to sleep. I always pay all your *fucking* bills." The last time he said fucking his neck tilted forward, his nose bumped her head, and his shouting sprayed her face.

Clara sat down on the floor, her lips thinning in a frown. He turned back to the television, his breathing hoarse with shouting. Suddenly she screamed, her hands clutched into fists, her arms flexing alongside her hips. You should marry me, she shouted. Marry me, marry me, marry me . . .

She rose to her feet, screaming, her elongated hands clutched tightly into powdered fists that never hit him, only ventilated the air around his shoulders and face. "¿No eres un hombre?" She answered her own question in the negative, her head swinging wildly on her stringy neck. No, you're not a man. You couldn't be. A man would know how to treat me right. "Tú, señorito, me tienes miedo. Te doy vergüenza." I frighten you, she said, I make you ashamed. The way you turn from me when those women come around: I can tell your shame. Even without speaking English, I can tell.

Stan lit a cigarette; he said, "Quit the big fucking drama."

Perhaps she only meant to knock the cigarette from his mouth, but he jerked as she came at him, and her hand made contact with his face. He tried to reach for her then, but as she backed away she stumbled on the magazine rack. He caught hold of a pleat in her skirt and heard it tearing. A silence followed, a lull brought on by the surprise. The need to touch her skin became so strong it choked him. She flailed and tossed and later thrust against his weight, his furious weight, screaming against his mouth, first for him to stop, then just for him.

———   ═══

When he got home from the airport a day sooner than scheduled, she wasn't back from work. He meant to surprise her, maybe scare her a little, if only to see her yelp and then burst into kisses and laughter. *How was Costa Rica? Did the* chicas *seduce you, or did they see my spell in that secret place on your body that I tattooed on you while you were dreaming?* In his fantasies she was always the limber, laughing girl he met in Cuba, though her laughter these days, like her body, was no longer gentle.

A letter sat on the coffee table, alongside a glass with drips of vodka and lemon and an ashtray full of cigarette butts, some with a woman's lipstick, some without. He recognized Clara's handwriting, a letter to her sister in Cuba. He knew he shouldn't read it, but he picked it up anyway. He read at first only with lazy curiosity, then fast and without understanding its meaning.

> Querida Lisa,
>
> You wouldn't believe it, but I met another man. I'm so in love, Lisita, so in love it makes me cry. When Stan wants sex now all I see is Carlos: Carlos's hand, Carlos's chin, Carlos's eyes the way he looks at me when he stretches near me on the bed. And I get sick, Lisa. I feel sick through and through. You wouldn't believe it, but with Stan, I get like when a spider is in your hair. When he touches me I want to scream sometimes. I want to punch him. But I have to be nice. Like that, Lisita. It's a torture to love one man and have to sleep with another. But Carlos, he only calls me when he wants to fuck. And Stan won't marry me, he won't even marry me. Carlos said I'd get the green card sooner for being Cuban than for marrying Stan, that's what he said. To hell with Stan. All he has on me is money. But don't worry for me, Lisa. You should know your sister by now. I'll take care of us somehow. I sent you toilet paper and shampoo and cough syrup for the baby. I know it isn't much, but that's all that fit in Stan's suitcase . . .

He read it again, this time slowly, and the meaning became so clear it was a stalagmite in his chest, preventing him from breathing properly. The letter slid from his hand, gliding across the tiles with a hushed, protracted sound. Vaguely, he understood that there were phone calls to make, arrangements to work out, possessions to be sorted out and gathered. He had his suitcase still unpacked in the hallway, his briefcase on the couch next to him. It would have been as easy as getting up.

His breathing was a noise, ungraceful and metrical.

Break something. Break something of hers.

He bolted to his feet and kicked at a chair. He knocked out a statuette of St. Barbara, taken by an easy rage. The porcelain shards skittered circularly across the tiled floor. He grabbed the top edge of a bookcase and brought it down, wincing at the noise it made as it shattered. He knocked the two glasses and the ashtray off the table and crashed his fist through the glass top. He felt pain in his hand, felt it travel up his arm and neck, surprising and strangely right, the pain clamping at his hand, the pain holding on to him.

He placed his hands on his hips and stopped. Panting. He could not understand why he did this. Everything lost, broken, scattered. He saw no sense in what he had just done, not even in the cracks of her black Santería candles. He stepped over the overturned bookcase, delicately, carefully, as if he were stepping between pieces of his own dismembered body, and reached under the shambles for his pack of cigarettes. He sat Indian style on the floor, inhaling the smoke and holding his hair with his hands, his temples pounding against his fingertips.

Clara. And another man. There she was in his head, the girl of his dreams. Dancing. She was a fish in the dark room, with the colored lights striking her skin, stripes of cobalt blue, vermilion, and emerald green. A colored fish in a tank, the girl. Then it wasn't a person he thought about but a mouth, a segment of a breast, her tight, powdered wrists, her smooth, creaseless forehead, and her wet mouth when he made love to her on the bathroom floor, slamming against her body so hard he thought he could hear her whimper.

"Stan!"

It came out of her mouth as a gasp. But after a moment she called his name again, calm and quietly angry. She held her hips with her hands and demanded, "¿Bueno?" What is this? "¿Bueno?"

"Carlos," he said.

He said it again, after a moment, the same way she had said *Stan* before.

She stared back at him, expressionless, and took off her red jacket. She was wearing red vinyl boots that matched her miniskirt and the thick red headband in her short hair. She sat and crossed her legs at the ankles. She was a candy cane, a sweet holiday treat.

Her face seemed to bend slightly, to soften in the light. There he was inside her brown eyes, a dark blur. His hands clenched together as if praying. There he was: two waxy shapes like candle stubs, one in each of her flat eyes.

He got up but stumbled instead to his hands and knees as if drunk. She got up and pulled down at her skirt. Her gesture, so pragmatic and self-oriented, made him lurch for the door. He stumbled out and down the stairway, his hand clamped around the banister as if that might save him, as if that might stop him from falling and falling into that hole he was falling through, had been falling into and through for hours.

He heard her steps fast behind him so he hurried, but he felt anchored to the ground somehow. He was heavy and falling at the same time. All things felt possible to him now: Clara fucking another man, and the letter, the letter he was not supposed to read, and falling, and feeling anchored, and falling at the same time.

"¡No vayas!" she cried, digging her nails in his arms. "Espera." Don't go. Wait.

Her voice exploded inside him like glass, and its shards cut his throat. Her fingers clung to his arm as he lurched down the steps. She was limber, her breasts brushing against his back. He managed the lobby with her still attached to his arm.

"No puedes dejarme," she pleaded. Don't leave me. You can't. "No puedes dejarme," she cried louder. "No puedes." Her hands took hold of a crease on his shirt. Her touch caused him pain, made him twist suddenly, reel to strike her with his words.

"It was never my intention to marry you. You're nothing but a low-class whore. I would never, ever marry you." Then he shouted all of that again in Spanish, not sure of the word for low-class and calling her instead a dirty whore twice.

Her mouth was a curved crease. She winced, her eyes blinking as he shouted. His intestines felt like sailor ropes, and that's how he knew; it would all die there in that nest of ropes in his stomach. He turned around. Her fingers brushed his elbows but did not hold him back.

"Aah, Stan," she sighed after him. He caught a glimpse of her reflection in the double glass doors. She had her hands on her hips. And she shook her head no.

"If it was me, I would call the police," Magda said. Her bangs were fixed in tiny colored rollers that clung to her forehead without pins. "But that's me. I'd get that bitch out of my house. Call the police. They'll deposit her Cuban ass on the next boat headed that way."

Magda's hips swayed gently as she wiped the kitchen counter. In Spanish they'd say, No tiene pelo en la lengua. She had no hair on her tongue, Magda. That was the Spanish way of saying she was a straight shooter.

Stan took a sip of his coffee. It felt watery and bitter in his mouth, and he hesitated, almost, to gulp it down. He didn't know if he was up for a straight shooter. The first time he fucked Magda there had been that surprise: it hadn't been so enthusiastic; it hadn't been quite as good as he thought it might be. She had been married twice, had three children from three different men. Once when he had been on a date with her, she had lured him out to the back of the nightclub, an urgency to her body that had touched him. They had made out strong against the recycling bin in the alley, her tongue tasting of menthol and vodka, a faint foulness of sweat mixed with her perfume. The sex was good. It wasn't amazing, but it was good. He came back for it now and again — the kitchen, the transparent dresses, the flickering, *hairless* tongue. Maybe more for the tongue than for the sex, the way she had of putting things in perspective, laying them on the line; sometimes he needed it.

"Just for the night," Stan said. He tried to guess which of Magda's kids drew the picture of the mountain and the hut. A bunny magnet held it stuck against the refrigerator door. He guessed maybe the youngest kid.

"You OK, baby?" Magda wiped her hands on her floral skirt. Then she was next to him, and her fingers, still damp, got tangled in his hair.

"Fine," he said into his coffee.

She lit a cigarette and dropped his lighter on the table as though she couldn't bother to let it back down gently. Two thick breaths of smoke broke against his face.

"I never knew what you saw in that bitch anyway." Magda swallowed the smoke this time, but it escaped in rivulets from her nostrils. "In Cuba she's a dime a dozen. But for you . . . Any skinny brown ass with an exotic label on it is a souvenir to show off to your buddies."

There was a moment of silence for which he was grateful. Then one of Magda's children shouted, "Captain Moron!" and the other two burst into giggles. Their voices came from upstairs. Stan could hear the television, some action figure commercial, then the trailer for a period movie.

"You wanna fuck?" Magda asked.

He didn't answer, but maybe an answer wasn't required. He may have nodded; he wasn't sure. Whatever he did, he did enough. She unbuttoned his shirt, her cigarette burning from the side of her mouth. He wasn't even required to hold her. His elbows were still on the kitchen table, his fingers still curled around the coffee mug.

Stan closed his eyes and let it out in a breath: his hurt, exhaustion from the trip, from shouting, from reading the letter *she'd* left so neatly, carelessly on the table. What she could have meant by leaving that letter right on the dining room table, an invitation for him to know, to really *know* — he couldn't imagine what. Magda moved her hands along his body. His muscles relaxed where her fingers touched but tightened again and tingled where her fingers left their imprints of warmth.

"Feel better, baby?"

He groaned, closed his eyes, tried to concentrate on the feel of Magda's lips. *She* was in his head. *She* had her fists closed tight and hitting his chest. *She* held her hips and shook her head no.

Magda's voice was throaty, honey-coated. "Let's go to the bedroom." Her hands held his hands, her face turned up toward the ceiling from where he could still hear music and voices, could still hear Magda's kids laughing. The kitchen light hit Magda's thin rayon dress so that her large breasts appeared clearly to him under the floral pattern: her nipples were wide stains, coffee brown. He felt no desire for her. No desire at all.

She pulled him onto the bed on top of her, and kissed him slow and patient on the mouth. Stan worked his mouth upon hers, eyes closed. In his head something was moving, the limbs of a beach pine wrestling with the wind. He touched Magda's sweat-damp skin, his hands tracing the curves of her long, slim body. He entered her slowly, struggling. Sand kicked up with the wind, scattering over the coast, flying into the sea.

"Will you go back to her?" Magda whispered.

"No." Stan said. He rested his head on the pillow and felt the tears spilling from under his eyelashes. Magda kissed him.

"Are you thinking about her?"

"No," he said.

"Do you think you will stay with me for a while?"

"Yes," said Stan. He whispered, "Yes."

She said, "Tell me again how it all happened."

The moonlight strikes the beach with strips of dancing shadows. Her short hair tosses with the wind. She smiles at him. She smiles. He does not try to pull away when her hand touches his neck. And later, when her dark lips make contact with the skin on his belly, he feels the pleasure like a needle, stitching his soul to her flesh, piercing him through and through.

She's Anonymous

I'd never thought I'd be looking for a date on the Internet, but something needed to be done. I'd found a note in my mailbox from my ex-husband's new girlfriend with a recipe for making candied walnuts and a thank you for the one-dollar Christmas tins I left behind. My ex, who is helping to raise her five-year-old daughter, wanted to know if I could do without the Christmas decorations, my apartment being so small and my having no family to celebrate with since my mother's death. I'm supposed to be happy, free in my thirties, no kids, a fun job, good health, but it hits me right in the gut. It's the way it is with me lately. One day I'm humming Broadway tunes from the moment I wake up, another day I lie on the couch, an open book resting on my chest, my eyes reading the bland, speckled whiteness of the ceiling as the meaning to my life.

I'm meeting my new date on the Hollywood broadwalk by the beach. The locals like to emphasize its being a *broad*walk rather than a *board*walk, as if wanting to claim some distinction for our sleepy Florida town against its garish California namesake. Every morning I walk along this very strip mall, in love with the melancholy features of its aged, mismanaged buildings, the constant bickering of parrots, the yell of sunburned children playing. It suits a gentler sort of folk, this place: Canadian families glowing on their wicker mats like cream cheese on crackers, senior citizen tourist groups meeting for dance classes, sun spots and veined legs quivering at the crack of dawn, and that handful of nostalgic locals like myself who are drawn to the water like turtles digging for nest holes in the sand. Tonight the moonlight softens the cracked pavement, the giddy laziness of weekends, and even the fine lines around my eyes, teenagers perched on the empty bandstand too easily pleased by the sight of my legs, shouting gawky overtures, mistaking me for someone much younger than myself.

Nick's, the bar where I'm meeting my date tonight, is on the least populated end of the strip, one side of it facing a parking lot, the other side open to the sand and sea. As I walk in, I'm greeted by a waft of smoke, the smell of whiskey, beer, maybe vomit. A man tucked in an oversized cowboy hat strums on a guitar, the stool he sits on wobbling over a dingy, wood-slatted stage where you'd expect glass shards from the last decade to be lurking in the cracks, waiting for a naked foot and a lawsuit.

I have a weekly column in the local paper, fun stuff to do in Broward County, Florida: the hot spots, new clubs, that kind of thing. Once I wrote about this bar: *It's where medieval cowboys would hang out if there had been a feudal period in Colonial Florida, bricks and crenellations on the rooftop like a medieval fortress left over from a Hollywood movie.* In spite of its rickety appearance, Nick's can get crowded on a weekend. I've never met Kyle before, and I'm worried that I won't recognize him when I see him. His picture in the Internet personals was confusing. His smile was strained. The light was bright. His hair looked yellow. In his email he said, No, not yellow. I have brown hair.

I wade through a crowd enveloped in country music, beer, and suntan lotion, and I notice someone looking at me, a young man. He stands up, tall, smooth, light-skinned, and sturdy—a beech tree.

"Kyle?" I ask.

He grabs my hand, shakes it, says, "No." He laughs and kisses me on the cheek.

"You don't look like your picture," I tell him. "I was worried I was coming on to a stranger."

"He'd have been pleased, I'm sure," Kyle says. He motions me to a seat and asks me if I want a drink.

I should say no. I'm a bad drinker. Fall on my back like nothing. But I'm reassured by Kyle's good cheer. He breathes color and noise, like a television set. I'm hypnotized.

I'll drink slowly, I tell myself.

———

I'm thirty-three years old this week, and this makes me eight years older than my date. Marriage isn't exactly the best prep work for dating. I don't even know where to start. I'm better with the written word than I am with the bar scene, so I went for the Internet first. Kyle's personal mentioned an interest in Otis Rush, Ayn Rand, and amateur poetry. It's the poetry part that got me to write. My ex-husband had read my column only once, said it bored him; it was kid stuff, he said. He dubbed it, Importing the California Myth.

"And they don't even give you credit for it," he accused me one time, pointing to the spot where my byline should have been.

"It's just a listing-type column," I explained. "At the bottom where they tell you where to fax or call for information, there is my name, see?"

He just grinned. The prosecution resting.

My column was no Pulitzer-winning writing, true, but for years I'd been working as the VP of marketing for a small catalog company, and my heart just wasn't in it. Taking the column was an offering to the goddess of the art. I thought if I could give up money and security, maybe someday she might give me back my poetry, the will to create. Back in college I had written a couple of dozen poems, but my husband didn't see them until we were at the therapist's office ten years later, and by then I just didn't write anymore. After the divorce I promised myself I'd at least have that to share with my next lover: the opera, the theater, music, books—stuff that stays.

"I don't meet anyone at work," I wrote in my first email to Kyle. "Are you really a poet, or is it just a line? Have you published anywhere?" I gave him a list of my small accolades: the *Forgotten Reader Review*, the *Crappy Quarterly*, the types of magazines that go out of business after the first issue and don't return their subscriber's money. Of course, I didn't tell Kyle that. I wasn't really after admiration for my dubious accomplishments. I just wanted to see if he was honest about his interests.

"I confess, all I write are songs on my guitar. Is that poetry?" he asked.

"It's art," I answered, and I meant it.

We exchanged stats after that, and that's when I found out he was barely twenty-five. I wrote him back immediately: "I'm older than you, but maybe we could still be friends. I know some pretty interesting clubs that host poetry readings and open mike nights. People do their act, they sing, rap, bang on congas, all sorts of crazy stuff."

He wrote back, "I would love to do that with you someday. It sounds like fun. And don't worry about the age difference. Anything could happen."

I can't say why, exactly, but it sounded gentle.

I take a look at my date tonight: eyes, Colorado backwoods in the fall. Big like a baby's. And the way he speaks into my hair, voice of a DJ on an easy-listening station. He can't sit still while he speaks, swaying just so, nodding his head or running his hand over the bar as though feeling for imperfections. It makes me think about what's inside him to make him move like that; it makes me want to peer into his thoughts. I have a feeling they are a rush of something powerful to sway him like that, like a river at high water.

He talks to me about having hiked the Appalachian Trail through three states, my imagination barely keeping up with the technical information he gives me about shells and fleeces and filters having failed their promised performances and the way these minor accidents add up to big trouble. I tilt my head back to drink his words, gobble up the fat of his adventure. He'd like to do the whole thing one day, he tells me, take off from work six months. That, and climb Denali in Alaska.

"You should do it as soon as you can," I tell him. "Don't wait. You spend most of your life at work. You have to do what makes you happy whenever you get a chance."

Kyle takes my hands and looks at each of my fingers, a smile at the side of his mouth making him look just a bit older, a bit more sophisticated.

"I have a feeling these hands haven't been kissed enough," he jests, kissing my knuckles. I smile at him, silly, through sips of my drink.

―――――

When a tree dies, it leaves its stump rooted deep into the earth. That's what it was like for my marriage. A tree can rot and rot for years. Leaves stop growing, flowers stop blooming, limbs crack and fall, but it takes an earthquake, a fire, or a hurricane to rip those roots out of the earth. When we were nineteen, having a similar CD collection meant that we were soulmates. Then we grew up. My husband didn't hit me or get drunk or waste his salary on gambling, and I didn't cheat on him or spend all our money on shoes, so we stuck it out, the way our parents taught us to, with that singsong about all-the-crazy-passion-stuff-fades-for-everyone clear in our minds. We looked at each other across the dinner table, straining for smiles, stumbling for things to say. It was like eating sandwiches dirty with sand—getting nourished all right, but all the taste spoiled by the grit. I looked at my girl-friends who were single, counting the days they had left to their next birthdays, talking about the shelf life of their eggs, smearing their mascara under their eyes after disaster dates, and I thought, Well, at least I'm married.

My husband and I lived separate lives under the same roof: he claimed the couch, I claimed the bed; he had control of the television set, I had unfettered use of the microwave; he lived in the guest room where he'd set up his office, I had the bathroom with the big tub, the kitchen, and most of the bedroom. In our last year we had even gotten into the habit of taking separate vacations: I at my mother's, where he refused to visit; he on men-only fishing trips. We were numbed by the slow tide of our compromises, shedding pleasures so naturally we never even noticed they were gone: first, control of our individual lives, then excitement in our conversation, then sex . . . By the eighth year of our marriage, kindness had given up on us both. By then, it almost seemed expected.

Kyle. Maybe it's his youth, his energy, the way he exudes willingness to live. I listen to him talk and I want to swallow the moon, feel pregnant with her borrowed light. I want to sing a song and belch out ribbons of her mystery.

"It's turtle-nesting season," he explains on the phone, his voice dropping to a whisper, a caress to my ear. "We could go watch the turtles on the beach after sundown if you want. It's not far from where you live."

We move slowly, on our knees, sand in our shoes, in the palms of our hands, tiny grains punching holes in our soft skin, adhering to our cheeks with the wet mist blown in from the shore. The turtles look like oval shadows, washing up pained and heavy on the beach. The rangers from the conservancy speak in hushed, almost sacred voices.

"There is only so much time before they can lay their eggs," a tall, sandy-blond woman tells us. Later she points at a dark blur by the edges of my field of vision. "Sometimes if the nests are unbalanced they will collapse with the weight of the sand. With boat propellers, pollution, and natural dangers acting against them, some of the turtles are so badly wounded that they are ineffective in their efforts. Still they will continue to dig through the night, and some of them die before they are able to deposit their eggs. Our volunteers here at the center are trained to monitor their progress. We have to be careful. If the turtles see us touching their holes, they will abandon the nest, regardless of how much they've dug, and start all over at another location. The work sometimes fatally exhausts them."

I catch a glimpse of a thick, low shadow struggling over the ridged and crested sand. In spite of the darkness, I imagine I can see the grooves of her strange skin, lines in her leathery green forming cryptic geometrical patterns. I feel awed by her awkward movements over the cold sand, by her stubborn persistence to ensure survival. How beautiful she seems in her enormous struggle against the unstable sand and her exasperating slowness.

Kyle squeezes my hand, puncturing me with the exhilaration of this night—a quick intravenous spurt of ecstasy.

Later we go to a bar on the pier. It's only our second date, and I'm drinking, drinking way too much. I know this and still I can't stop it. Within moments I'm falling off my stool, braying out my laughter like a donkey.

"I'm not a drinker," I tell Kyle. I have no faith that he'll believe me. He keeps buying me the gin, the tonic getting thinner.

We sit by the water, overlooking the intercoastals. The woodboard creeks with the slapping of water. When I see the surface break, a ripple of white spray, I think about a manatee coming up for air, waiting out her extinction, braving the threat of propellers for a leaf or a piece of lettuce.

"Would you like to kiss me?" Kyle asks. It catches me by surprise.

I want him to like me, so I say, "I think I've wanted to kiss you since I first saw you tonight." I don't even think it's true, but I say it. I make it true.

"Why don't you kiss me now?" he says.

The breeze in South Florida is like a slut breathing between my legs. It blows sweat on my skin, wet and naughty.

Once it starts I can't stop it. I lean into the kiss, cover his lips with mine. I live the kiss. I suck the sweetness out of every contact. I take his tongue into my mouth; I give him mine. With my fingertips I feel the bones of his shoulder; I feel the curve of his muscles. His fingers are long and slender. He's a musician, hands that know just where to touch. I take his face into my hands and offer him me, with my mouth, my tongue and teeth. It's all here. I take his hand and place it over my breast, guide his palm over my nipple and down to my belly, show him my geography, know where he can find me.

He drags a hand through his hair, and says, "I feel so good."

Inside the bar, a man is looking at us, drink in hand, eyes gleaming. I see myself through this stranger's eyes, and in my drunkenness I form the faint idea that maybe, just maybe, I can be swallowed by the sacred fire, that all the tales of love are true, not just for strangers but for myself as well.

Kyle teases me, brushes his mouth against mine, but pulls back just as I try to kiss him.

"I want to hear you say it," he whispers.

I try again for his mouth, but he moves back just barely, just enough.

"Tell me," he demands, his voice low, almost hoarse.

I realize, suddenly, what it is that he wants to hear.

"I want to fuck you." I bite my lips saying it. It's the word *fuck*, the way it hits my lips. I've never been so generous to my desires, so honest to my wants. "I want to *fuck* you, Kyle."

Within moments we're stumbling out of the bar, toward the beach. I'm unzipping his pants behind some bushes.

I'm not this woman. I'd like to tell him this, but it's pointless. I could stop it all now. *I'm not this.*

Then we're in his car. He's driving and I have his penis in my mouth. We stumble up the stairs to his place, locked-in and twisted on each other. We hit the bed so hard I think the springs will collapse. I open up, this strange flower. Who is this woman? He penetrates me and I push my head back, I grab and twist the sheets, I writhe like a whore. I'm loving it. I've never been this. I don't know who I am.

The therapist says, "You can't fight it all by yourself. You're in denial. It'll catch up to you, sooner or later."

She's worried about me, my therapist. She thinks my mother killed my marriage.

My mother died less than a year ago. A phone call came from New York, from the minister, and then someone else, I don't know who, asked me questions I barely understood. What kind of flowers for the casket? What kind of music for the wake? It was death, seeping into my life: stink from the muck.

Even later, back in Florida, death was still on me, clinging to my clothes like New York winter. Every waking moment, everything I did, my mother was in the casket, looking as though she could almost breathe if someone would just pinch her.

I was alone at the funeral. For my husband, the alibi was the new job. It was his training. It was a meeting with a very important client. I shook hands, accepted sympathies, endured the full length of a Catholic mass. I was going to make it all right. Then, the burial. My mother's one hundred and forty-two pounds made a dull noise when the casket hit the ditch, a muffled kind of thump, no resistance. And me? I don't know. They said I screamed. I don't remember. I should have felt relieved. From now on, all the talking between us would be poured over a stone, useless as before, but final. We'd never understood each other, and there wasn't going to be any more tries at it.

When I came back to Florida, my husband sat in front of the TV, not looking at me. I tried to talk about it. I was crying, standing in the living room, barefooted. He hadn't wanted to discuss the funeral at all. He'd talked about the way his meeting went, looking straight ahead. He never noticed my crying.

"Go lie down," he said. "You're just tired. Go to bed."

It took another week for me to find that blouse in the laundry hamper. Ann Taylor. I was almost relieved. For days it didn't seem to mean a thing. Another shred to emphasize the rubble that our life had become. There was the lawyer to think about, the separation of the assets, canceling the health insurance, renting the moving truck.

Then one day I sat down to think about it: When did it happen? Where was I? Where have I been while it all happened, all of it, where?

The coffin trapdoor opens and my mother's corpse, tight in a sack, hits the cold ground with a thump. He clenches her breasts and slides his hands, gentle, to her crotch.

I wake up four hours into my sleep, my heart beating so fast it's like a fluttering of some sort, some lung-bat lost in my body cavities.

Kyle sits next to me at the piano. He shows me how to play a pentatonic scale. He says he doesn't play, but his fingers are confident and agile over the keys. He dictates the notes to me like someone who's had no training. He says, "Two notes up, and then the third black note, and fourth white note." He can't say three halftones higher or even E flat and G. He doesn't know what that might be on the piano.

I keep laughing, banging on the keyboard, Kyle guiding my hands as though he really knows. He says, "You're so, so lovely," says it in the middle of a sentence when I don't expect it. "Play it like I showed you," he says, as if nothing.

I play a whole pentatonic scale, first in A, then in C. He insists enough that I agree to play a blues progression for him while he solos on his acoustic. As a teenager in school I had tried to play for a jazz ensemble, but I could barely keep up with just the basic score. My training was in classical: every note dictated, every pause accounted for. Something like my life.

"Where were you when I was in high school?" I ask Kyle, my fingers finding the notes with more confidence than before.

"Grade school, I think?" I can tell from the way his mouth curls at the side that he means it as a joke, but I feel like I've just tried to drink icy water too fast.

My mind is peopled with my past. Mother, husband, the enemies and friends I've had and lost, the imaginary lovers that came to me when I slept with my husband, lovers I had before I married whose life I might have had . . . they sit inside the folds of my eyes. The things they've said are noises in my head. I see their faces when I go to sleep, warped by faulty memory, my imagination drawing in the missing details. I talk through them when I imitate their gestures, repeat the things I learn from them, ghosts I invoke like a voodoo witch. How have they possessed me?

"Keep talking," I tell Kyle, fingers falling on skin like petals. I straddle him, I hold his hands, take his fingers in my mouth.

"I don't even remember ever living with my father," he says. "I was two years old when he left . . ." I gobble it up. Morsels of Kyle. I try them in my mouth, I roll them on my tongue. The bittersweet taste of him. ". . . If you think I should try talking to him after all that . . . I don't think he realizes that anything he does affects me . . ." I move my hips slowly over his. Rhythms of pain, shocks of pleasure. The way his lips hang as if surprised. "I think . . . now . . . or it's going to be too late . . ." and then explosions of something, flesh crashing against flesh, a rush of blood, a gasp, strange country here, nothing legit, nothing too terribly clear.

After the sex I watch him dress. It happens accidentally, something I say, a joke: "No, it wasn't me; it must have been your other girlfriend." And just like that, a sour subject rises out of a casual conversation and takes on a life of its own. The women, the ghosts of his past, they populate the air between us like an invocation gone awry. All at once, unseen and unexpected, they seep out of his mouth, toxic presences infecting his words, seeking abode in my lungs.

His face is veined, cold, like marble. He's a chiseled stone. He sits on my chaise longue, hands crossed over his chest. I sit on the bed across from him, my hands on my knees. We are opposite shores of the same river.

He leafs through the catalog in his head: Jane, the high school girl who wouldn't French kiss. Susana with the blond hair and the pigtails, whom he'd been in love with since grade school. Tammy, who cried in his arms at the airport, then disappeared without a word. Jessica, the sexiest, who rode on his lap and screwed him as he drove. Then he mentions one more. Her spirit is so great that when she comes, she swallows all the others.

The details of her become bruised, strained like the thinness of his voice, the struggle of his words: "No, I never saw it coming. I thought we were perfect . . . Even when I begged her not to . . . she just kept walking . . . I'd been waiting for Valentine's Day, never got to ask her. I could have swallowed the ring I bought for her . . ."

Afterward, he becomes the man I've met, the Kyle lurking in beach bars and clubs, effaced by smoke and drink, limping behind his charm and jest.

"What was her name?" I ask. He shakes his head and says, "It doesn't matter."

I think about the sacred mystery of God's true name and the lore of ancient Greece, claiming that to know a creature's secret name was to hold its power.

Kyle looks at me in silence, waiting, and in his face I see the image of my husband as he stood the day I moved out, holding on to the handle of my suitcase, saying nothing.

Kyle: he breathes grief, lets his skin sport the blue tones of his loss. Kyle emanates all the colors, passion purple, backwoods green. His pain is so deep that it touches me. And I'm struck by the notion that if Kyle can redeem his love, he will have the power to free me. Real love is without expectations, I tell myself. I will be purged by my act of selflessness.

"You should talk to her," I tell him. Maybe I'm imagining that if I can redeem his mistakes, someone in a life that seems as far away to me as the lore of Greece will return the favor, and I will have back the love I gave up too soon when I stopped trying to love my husband. Or maybe I'm hoping that Kyle will understand why I'm doing this, and that will make him love me. It is futile, and yet the hopefulness in this gesture is so pure that it seduces me. It is as bright and noble as the Holy Grail of Kyle's love for his anonymous girlfriend.

Kyle crosses his arms as if to protect himself from my redemption plans. "She's living with another man," he says.

"Talk to her anyway," I say.

"You think she'll feel better knowing I'm still waiting for her?"

"Is she feeling bad about something? This is about you, Kyle. Not about her."

He takes a book from the nightstand near my bed, flips the pages as if looking for particles of what he's lost in there. He turns it over in his hands, breathing from his nose, a bull, a wounded bull in a corral, his hurt around him like barbed wire.

"Kyle, you have things to say that are sitting inside you, making you sick. You have to let her know."

Kyle clenches his hand into a fist. When he finally looks at me he says, "You're beautiful. If I were anyone but myself, I would love you."

My feelings are paper, crackling in the inside of his palm.

———

I talked to my mother on the phone a month before she died. I was pissed broke. She said she felt sick and wanted me to visit her. She always complained about feeling sick. She had been complaining about it for twelve years. She wasn't in good health, but her situation had been like that for years. Maybe next month, I told her.

"I have no money now. My *dearest husband*, he spends all night out with his friends, then he's too tired in the morning to go to work. We think he's going to get fired again."

"Of course," she countered, her voice a strange, bitter twang. "You're never at home, working, going to the gym, writing for that silly paper. You don't pay enough attention . . ." My life reduced to an old radio recording: I should have married a more stable man; I should have been a housewife, not a career woman; I should have had children right away; I should have been a different person; I shouldn't have been me; I simply shouldn't have, not at all . . . "Every man cheats. Every man will sleep with a whore now and again. It's not such a big deal. Look at your dad. We've been together thirty-five years."

"You and Dad have been fighting for thirty-five years."

I can still hear her breathing on the line awhile, refusing to get discomposed. "Well, at least I have someone to fight with." Then out of nowhere, she cries, "No, not another month. I can't wait another month."

Kyle calls me after a basketball game. "I'm mad as hell that the Heat lost. God, I can't believe, again! I won five dollars at poker, though. Whoo hoo! Why don't you send me to hell?" he shouts into the phone. "It's two in the morning. Why don't you hang up on me? I'm bothering you, aren't I? I woke you up." His voice spirals higher, sounding more and more like an apology.

"I'm not going to hang up on you, Kyle."

"I just wanted to hear a friendly voice."

"I know." We breathe on the line. Like something meaningful. He says, "Can I come over, now?"

I could hang up. I could crawl under the sheets, do what I was doing before he called, seeing my mother's corpse in the sack, feeling the bat in my rib cage.

I greet him at the door in a silk camisole. Kyle kisses me like in a romance novel, sometimes gentle, sometimes biting pieces of my soul from my lips. He holds me down to the mattress, he pins me with his weight, his fingers clasping tight around mine.

"When I look at you," he says, shaking his head as if it's something bad. He says, "So sexy." He trails off with a hiss. He holds my waist, he touches my face, he pulls a strand of hair off of my forehead. "It's rapture," he says.

I know better than to believe him, but I want it to be true, and so I don't hold back. I will be punished for this, I know, but right now I feel Kyle, I feel the hope. He will love me, I tell myself.

Kyle lifts my legs, holds my knees under his arms. I squeeze him between my thighs. His hands knead my breasts. I want to scream. I want to kick and gasp and twist and hold him down to me, hold him down so he won't go.

"Oh God," I whisper. The bed board bangs against the wall. "Oh God, oh God, oh God."

He calls me mostly in the middle of the night.

What are you wearing? Are you in bed? Can you come over?

I am controlled by my need, a harness sitting tight around my ribs, a bit in my mouth: Kyle, the sex, this strange closeness. But the spirit of the vengeful god haunts me. I can't forget her, the woman without a name. I want to know all about her, what she ate, what she wore, what was the tone of her voice when she gasped out her baby-doll yawns. I believe that what people yearn for in love is to have their lives made numinous by the immortal vision of their gods. And her name is so great, like the name of a goddess: it can't be spoken. Not in his presence, anyway.

"You've never told me her name." I dare ask only after sex, when he's least vulnerable. "That woman you loved . . ."

He shakes his head. "I've told no one."

"Why?"

He won't answer that, but he says, "She was so beautiful," holding his fingers to his forehead, as though the memory of her is a tumor. "And she was talented. Played the violin. The most talented woman I ever met."

"Have you never read my column?" I cross my legs, pull a cotton sweater over my naked breasts. He taps a cigarette on the coffee table and asks me if I want something to drink. As he pours water in a glass in the kitchen, I hear him talking, his back to me.

"I just don't think it's going to be anything more than sex between us," he says.

I go to him, wrap my arms around him from behind, my cheek against his back.

"It's not your fault," he says.

My marriage. If I trace it back, I can see where it started: bachelor party, the stripper leaving a thong bikini under the armrest, her calling card, her warning.

"It's part of the act, leaving something behind," my husband explained. "We were just partying, girl. Nothing bad."

Often I'd find things missing: earrings, shirts, a favorite miniskirt.

My mother used to hide her things so well she'd hide them from herself; then she'd blame my father, or the gardener, or the maid, or the neighbors' children who in her mind had snuck into the house when she was napping. It got worse with her illness. The look on her face when my father found her things, her zephyr ring, her grandmother's brooch, wrapped in silk and tucked into a corner under the mattress, wrapped in newspaper and flat under the picture frame. Her lips would curl back from her teeth, her hands shaking. "You hid them from me!" she'd cry. "You all want me to think I'm a lunatic."

I talked to my husband casually about the missing things. "I could have sworn . . . I'd only just worn it Friday . . ."

"Keep looking," he'd say. "It must be somewhere."

In the last year of our marriage I'd found T-shirts, blouses, a pair of nondescript panties that seemed just a bit too small. I found them in the laundry room, fallen behind the dryer or directly in the hamper. There was even a shirt on a hanger in my closet.

"What's this?" I held it up, examining it like a specimen. The things I'd find, they were never something I could have sworn I hadn't bought years before, forgotten by disorder and confusion. The image of my mother hovered in the back of my eyes, that silent threat. Only that blouse, that purple blouse. Ann Taylor. I took a harder look, the answer, so simple, already there: I never wore size four.

Most people accept it: their affairs become routine, their surreptitious passions stuffed in the closet when worn out like old, cherished clothes that fit no more. Counselors, friends, and relatives excused it: "It happens to everyone. Passion is for kids. Cheating means nothing. It's just sex." But for me, it was as if a pretty poster with a hologram was doused in gasoline and set on fire: I saw it all crumple before my eyes, that wonderful illusion, consumed, reduced to smoke and ashes. I prided myself on being a realist. There were no handsome princes to be had, no fairy-tale endings. I had friendship; I had companionship; I had someone I cared about whom I could count on. I mocked the quixotic foolishness of my romantic friends and exchanged it for what? A projection of a being, no more real than an interactive computer program, a character I created out of my needs and fears, the real man as unknown to me as the marriage I lived. I drop to my knees thinking about it, my hands in prayer to whatever is out there, God, this universe, a world of spirit who watches my mistakes, who laughs at the stupidity of my choices. I can live with anything, but let it be real, God, let it be mine.

I throw on a tight shirt and a pair of jeans, out to the bars, to ready sex. I revel in the errors and flatteries, like shots of tequila—highs that wear off quickly.

"My guess is, you're twenty six."

"Late twenties?"

"May I see your ID, miss?"

I'm a retired diva. I'm giving up the act; I throw my arms open and articulate my drama: "I'm thirty-three. The age of Christ. Good-looking enough to fuck but too worn-out to love."

They go through me like water, the nights of sex, the phone calls that aren't returned, the times I wait sitting on my bed, dressed up, lipstick in place, knowing I'm being stood up but still stubborn enough to hope. Clues in the restaurants where they take me, clues between the drinks and the appetizers.

"My last girlfriend was thirty. She was hunting. Anyone might have done for her, so long as it was marriage."

I sit across from my dates in restaurants, in bars, in quiet dinners at someone's condo, and I want to scream, "I'm not what you think." But I see them, so fixed in their beliefs, no different from Kyle, centered in his devotion to a nameless ghost. I'm not a fool to debate with an echo. I run up my dates' tabs with gin and tonics. I empty out their wallets and their scrotums.

Then one night I find myself alone in a gaudy beach club, my date having stumbled off to the dance floor after an overdose of whiskey and soda. I sit at the bar by myself, ignoring the obscene overtures of a prematurely balding man who is stuffed too tight in a cinnamon business suit. He sits with a group of fortyish-looking men who seem to have just been released from a marathon conference meeting at the penthouse of a towering, glass-paneled office building. I spy their movement for a while through the opaque mirrors behind the bar. They shout loudly, drip drink on the fancy ties they have impatiently loosened around their silk shirt collars. They make embarrassing comments to the too young/too eager waitress who shimmies her hips and breasts shamelessly for their guilt tips. I see myself reflected in the movements of this other contingency: the gray-haired men, balding, faded business shirts and wrinkled slacks that are bruised around the knee. They carry their baggage on their clothes, mingling surreptitiously through the nightclub crowds, the fashions they don't understand, the hip-hop they despise: stalkers in the jungle. They laugh too loud about getting in shape, their hairy hands slapping their bulging bellies. Am I one of them? I ask myself. Just wearing a prettier mask?

———————

I have a comfortable couch, a twenty-four-inch television, and a Japanese VCR. I watch the same movies over and over again, forgetting the ones I rented, renting them again, watching them not so much for their predictable story line as for the noise, the music, the enactment of emotion that seems so safely distant, so soothingly comprehensible.

I hear the phone ring, but I don't get up to get it. I'm certain it's a mistake. It is well past midnight, and only Kyle would call so late. Kyle who doesn't call anymore. Kyle who has exhausted every interest in me, even in sex.

I try not to think about it, but my heart feels like it's beating in my throat. The phone rings again and again, as if unwilling or too stubborn to give up. I tiptoe my way to the caller ID, holding my breath, as if it will stop ringing if I am too loud, stop being who I think it might be.

I pick up, finally, my hand trembling, my voice negotiating words through the odd beating of my heart.

"Is it you?"

Kyle doesn't respond for a few seconds, breathing on the line as if surprised. I hear him sniffling. Maybe he has a cold. Or maybe— the thought hits me like a kick in the ribs—he's been crying. Finally he says, "It's me."

All at once I want to say, Where have you been? What took you so long? Why did you stop calling me? Kyle, you bastard, come on over right now. Instead I wait for him to say something. He breathes on the line, content to have me on the phone. The silence enervates me, teases me, tortures me. I fear that if it goes on long enough, he will hang up.

"I'm sorry . . ." I start to say, then try to think for what. For wanting him so much? "I'm sorry that I was such a melodramatic bitch."

He ignores my verbal fumbling and says, "I'd like to see you."

I check my makeup in the rearview of my car before hurrying out to Nick's, cursing myself for the extra twenty minutes I took in setting up my hair for Kyle who might not wait for me, Kyle who might slip away as quietly as he did before.

But I see him sitting at the bar in front of the television set, right at the same place he sat where we met the first time. His hair is so much longer since I last saw him that I barely recognize him. There's that same cowboy singer, that same basketball game on television.

"It's you," he says when I sit next to him, wiping a bead of whiskey from his lip.

"I didn't recognize you either," I joke. "Thought I was coming on to a stranger."

"He'd have been pleased, I'm sure," Kyle says. It's the same thing he said that first night, but he doesn't kiss me on the cheek. He doesn't order a drink for me. We sit in silence for a while, except for an occasional comment about women he sees strutting out on the broadwalk, angels glowing with the glare of street lamps, moon shadows in the breeze, and rustling palm leaves. "Now, that blond. That one is my type."

"So how come you called me?" I ask him. He glances at me like a Polaroid snapshot, taking me in and spitting me right out before I'm even in focus. I notice redness around his eyes. I know him well enough to realize he's been crying.

"I was at a party, but it ended early."

"Is that all?"

He shrugs, accepts a shot he must have ordered before I got there, gulps it down. "Naw, I've just been feeling melancholy, that's all."

I touch his arm, and he leans his cheek on my hand. We're this bedraggled couple, sitting knee to knee, glossy and tight on the outside, shattered and brittle on the inside. Painted husks.

"Come home with me," he says.

"Kyle . . ." I protest, but he puts his lips over mine, and I feel that stupid hope surging in me, his sadness calling me as though I have the power to heal him.

We drive to his place, a comfortable quiet between us. Below the bridge, the moonlight pelts the water like a phosphorescent rain. I unroll the window, feel that wet breeze clinging to my skin, this Florida air, so thick with sea balm and salt, as tangible as the yearnings that won't let go.

At his place, Kyle shows me a picture of his last climbing adventure. Mount Washington.

"It's not Denali, not yet. But I'm getting there," he says with a grin, handing me over the glossies. He looks happy for the first time tonight. I look at the frigid emptiness of the landscape bleeding through the 4 x 6. Rough crags and ice formations. An open, steel-colored sky sitting like a lid over the wind-gnarled mountain. Kyle himself appears in the pictures only once, minute by contrast, bundled in fat layers of almost useless clothing, his eyes barely visible, his copper beard glowing in the exaggerated brightness of a warmthless sun. He's clinging to the summit post, his body twisted to fight a gust of wind. I feel it going through me, that stinging pain, bullying paralysis to all the body's extremities, that bite of cold, that sensation of freezing away alive.

I try to shake it off, handing the pictures back to Kyle. "Why do you do this?"

He shrugs, glancing down at the pictures, something in his face like regret. "I don't know," he says. "It's hard."

"Yeah. Awful. It's so desolate and barren."

"I don't even think about where I am," he says. "It's just the trail, where I'm going to step, if I should use my rope, my cleats, if I should drink more water or save the filters. It's survival."

He sits down and picks up his guitar and strums, strums gently on a note or two, plucking the strings. Over the music he says, "If you have it in you, you know? To just get through it." I get the sensation he's not talking to me or, anyway, not about what I understand. Every time he pinches a note from the strings, I feel it on my skin. He plays a blues song, then riffs right into another. His fingers move solicitously over the neck of the guitar. He's like a lover, his cheek close to the heart of his beautiful instrument. I am caressed by a veil of tenderness for him, empathy for his pain, his stubborn love, and my own desire to be near him. I inch closer to him on the couch, but he crosses his legs, his shoes sticking out from under his knees. I can't get close to him. I look at him, waiting for him to meet my eyes, to understand what I want. His face is peaceful in a shadow of self-contained grief. He is beautiful, and strange, and perfect. Not at all like his picture, clenched against the wind, his hands tight around the summit post. Yet he is the same. In his voice I hear the woman, the anonymous muse. He holds on to her with her name; he makes her altar on the inside of his ribs, his private goddess. He claims the summit of cold and jagged mountains in her honor. And she, she becomes the shape of his words, the sound of his music.

Kyle looks at me as he sings a passage, his eyes looking straight into my eyes. He tilts his eyebrows, as if surprised and stunned by the green inside my irises. Kyle the gentleman. Kyle the charming jester. But I see his gaze fly beyond me, nesting into the varnished image of her. It's the same later, when he holds me in his arms. And when he closes his eyes to kiss me, I know I'm not there at all.

I let Kyle walk me to the car, and then I hold on to him, the length of my body pressed against his. I peck the tip of his ear, the awareness of this being our last time together heavy in my belly. "I'm sorry I couldn't cheer you up."

I feel his hands, open and warm against my back. "Did you try?" he asks. "Did you really, really try?"

I press my cheek against his and I hold on to my breath for a second, for Kyle, his essence fastened to my lungs. I feel him now, his aftershave in my hair, his forearms locked around my waist. I concentrate on the moment, memorizing all the details. Then, deliberately, I let him go. I can still feel him behind me as I enter my car, still feel the silhouette of him in the muggy night as I pull out of the driveway. His hands in his pants pockets. His legs just slightly open. At that curb. He'll be there for years.

I drive across the bridge and to the parking lot of my building. I walk to the docks and along the peer, toward the beach. I walk my bones all the way to where the water swallows the sand, heavy with Kyle, weighted with his scents and touches. My feet founder in the sand, and I stop to listen to the ocean, to the slapping of the wind against my ears. Off beyond the dune grass, the turtles dig their nest holes. I can see the silhouettes of volunteers as they crawl on their hands and knees and stealthily flatten the walls of defective nests.

Though I can't see them, the turtles dig, tired from the swim, sick with pollution. They lift their wary leathery heads, their dinosaur heads, to the same palpable darkness in which I breathe. They will be tired. They will be drunk with urgency and pain. Their moss green faces will rise in warning against the small white hands that try to help them.

A Rafter
in Miami Beach

The year Elizabeth moved to Miami Beach the Art Deco district was mottled with Cuban minimarkets where they sold *café con leche*, *tamales*, and *empanadas*, and where old men and young children sat under large ceiling fans, watching Spanish soap operas or listening to Latin jazz. There was a hair salon near Ana's Mini Market on the corner of Collins and Indian Creek, and there Elizabeth did manicures and washed hair for the Cuban women who liked to talk about their husbands and fathers who had been lawyers and doctors in the old Cuba.

The women at the salon loved to talk about politics when they weren't talking about their husbands.

"Castro es un asesino," they said when Elizabeth did the pedicures.

"No Castro, no problem."

They sold bumper stickers like that in Little Havana even in the supermarkets, and many of the cars that Elizabeth saw parked on the beach had them.

Some of the regulars at the hair salon talked often about their rich heritage. Some had told Elizabeth that they were Jewish; they had settled in Cuba during World War II, and they said that their fathers and grandfathers had come from Spain.

"Spain is my mother country, and I will always feel affection for it," one would say. "But I will never forgive the Spanish government for welcoming that pig Castro, who is a murderer and a thief . . ."

The women went on and on, as Elizabeth filed their nails and gave the ladies French-style manicures. Once in awhile she'd gaze and looked awestruck at the women who spoke. She wished that she could walk into a salon and say such strong things as these women said, and know about Castro, and know all about her ancestors. People always seemed to know so much. Elizabeth wished she were more cultured.

The regulars at the parlor had a strong sense of patriotism. They had lived on the beach for twenty-five years, some of them even longer, but they spoke Spanish better than English, and they still ate *guayaba* and fried plantains and knew the words to Ruben Blades when they played his songs on the cassette player that Marta's cousin had given to Maria, who owned the salon.

Marta's mother had known Maria's family in Cuba, and that is how Maria had gotten the funding to open up the salon. The Cuban family in Miami had all chipped in until Maria had enough capital for a big down payment and to qualify for a loan.

Elizabeth sometimes thought about that, trying to picture the families in Cuba who all knew each other. She had seen bits and scraps of Cuba in the picture books they sold on Lincoln Road in South Beach and in the news on the Spanish channel, but most of what she had in her head about Cuba was pure imagination. She pictured narrow streets, and great big ancient buildings, and spacious houses with dusty doorsteps and wooden shutters, and old toothless men with large straw hats drinking black coffee in the shade of ancient mango trees.

She thought maybe that women hung their clothes on rope lines and gossiped to each other, shouting from their windows across the alleys. That is why they all knew each other, she supposed. Havana must have been a small and neighborly place.

Elizabeth wasn't Cuban. She wasn't even Hispanic. In fact, she hardly spoke more than a word or two of Spanish, all that she had learned in high school. She was actually from Somerville, New Jersey, and she was American, with Irish and Dutch blood. Beyond that, Elizabeth didn't know a thing about her ancestry, except that Grandpa Hans, who had owned the bar in Princeton and who had died choking on his own vomit before Elizabeth was born, had been the first of her family to move to New Jersey from Pennsylvania.

"Why didn't anybody know?" Elizabeth had asked.

"Honey, you didn't talk to Grandpa Hans unless you had to."

Elizabeth was greatly embarrassed that she knew nothing about her family, and she hated it when people asked her where she was from. Sometimes she lied and said that she was Guatemalteca, a word that she had learned to pronounce almost flawlessly. She said to those who asked her that she never learned Spanish because her mother had wanted her to blend in with Americans and had never taught her to speak or told her anything about Guatemala. That story was far more interesting than the boring truth about being an American from New Jersey with ambiguous Dutch-Irish ancestry.

Guatemalteca. She liked the word, the way it sounded in her mouth, with the clipping of the *t*'s and the *c*'s drumming on her palate.

"Oye, guajira, ¿qué tu haces? I told you to sweep up all this hair. Now, come on, honey, I got Ana with the perm, and she gonna burn up on me."

"Sorry," Elizabeth muttered, rushing for the broom. She loved the clipped sounds of Maria's voice, that Hispanic heritage seeping through every word. She loved the way the words rippled in high and low pitches, almost like music, sounding beautiful and benevolent even when they were rebukes.

"¿Qué le pasa a la muchacha?" Ana asked.

"She got a new boyfriend and she's whupped."

"Ahh, a new boyfriend," Ana oozed, very interested. "And what's his name? *Como es que* ju don't tell us?"

Elizabeth giggled.

"Rueda," she said shyly.

"¿Rueda? ¿Qué clase de nombre es eso?"

"No hablo español."

"Ay, chica, what kind of name is Rueda? It no sound like a Christian name."

"His name is Rafael Rueda, but everyone calls him Rueda."

"Ah, Rafael. Cubano?"

"Aha."

"Good boy? Good family?"

"I think so. He's a writer."

"Aaah, a writer," the women chimed simultaneously.

Now the parlor knew about Elizabeth's new boyfriend; all the ladies were going to give her advice now or talk about the third cousin or nephew or uncle who had written a book in Cuba.

"My nephew is a journalist for the *Wall Street Journal*," one of the matrons said.

"My daughter worked for the *Miami Herald*, did I ever tell you dat?" someone chimed in.

"And my niece won the poetry prize when she was only five years old."

Elizabeth loved that the Hispanic women talked so loud to each other, and what they said all seemed raw and honest. They were a gaggle of benevolent mothers and grandmothers.

Back in New Jersey, when her dad was still around and when the family was forced to spend an evening or even an hour together, the conversations had been laconic and full of superficial pleasantry.

"And how is the work on the garage coming, Jim?"

"Oh, just fine, Lily. I should be done about next week."

"Oh, that's wonderful, just splendid. And how about you, Elizabeth? How is school?"

"I hate it. I think I am going to drop out," she had said once, just to see what would happen. But Aunt Lily just nodded and smiled and said, "That's wonderful." That's when Elizabeth knew that no one was listening.

In Elizabeth's home, what was important foremost was to pretend that everyone was having a perfectly splendid time. Then one evening it was seven o'clock and Daddy hadn't come home from work. He called from a gas station at nine that same night and said he had never been happy, was suffocating, had to take a chance in life, and then he wasn't Daddy anymore, he was "Jim," and all men were pigs, and no one was allowed to talk about Jim except to say that everything awful that had ever happened to the family had been his fault.

"Your mother needs her space," Lily explained. "She needs to be left alone."

Everyone up north liked to say things like that, needing space, needing to be left alone. Left alone. It was a scary combination of words, incredible to think that someone might actually desire such a state of being. That expression wasn't used like that in the Spanish language. Elizabeth knew because she had asked Nino, at Ana's Mini Market, who always made her *café con leche* strong and with one sugar, just the way she liked it.

"We say, like, déjame en paz. But if you translate literally, it dos no mean leave me alone. It means, like, leave me in peace. Los gringos, you like to say tings like dat, but no Latinos. We more friendly like dat. We more like to talk about peace. Who wants to be alone, no?"

"Couldn't agree with you more, Nino," Elizabeth had said, paying for her coffee with the bus money. She had walked home that night. It wasn't really a far walk, from Collins to Alton Road, and it was actually very pleasant in May, with a cool breeze blowing from the beach. To the right of her down to 23rd Street the Intracoastal causeways opened wider, and the Art Deco buildings, the houses of the millionaires, and the hedges and palm trees flanked the banks. There were still a few speedboats scudding fast across and the slower water taxi bringing happy tourists from one end of South Beach to the other.

Elizabeth decided to take the scenic route, through Collins and up Lincoln Road mall, wanting to see the lean, tanned, young people on roller blades, zooming past the art galleries, and the House of Beads, and the Allied Movie Theatre, which played only foreign films and movies by gay directors. And then of course there were the cafes: Gertrude's and Van Dyke's two of her favorites, tables and chairs sprawled on the paved avenue, where the waitresses who claimed they had just moved down from New York bustled with trays of fat-free pies and mocha cappuccinos.

The night she met Rafael Rueda there had been a poetry reading at Books and Books. Elizabeth had never actually been to a poetry reading. That was the kind of thing done by people who went to college. But the applause had drawn her, so she began to pay attention. Some of the poems were good and it was like listening to music. Others were strange, and she couldn't understand them, but she could feel the enthusiasm of the writers, and their eyes seemed to sparkle when they talked to each other about this one's talent and that one's work, and the electricity of the event moved her.

"Have you brought a poem or a story to read?" someone asked.

Elizabeth had burst out laughing. "Oh, I'm not a writer. I'm a beautician."

Quick smile. Sparkle inside dark eyes.

"An honest one, at last. You think anyone here's a writer?" A dark mass of curls swung as the head of the man speaking to her turned toward the reading poet and then back to her. "Crap. Maudlin, oral masturbation of pretentious people without jobs."

"I think it's exciting," Elizabeth had said. "I think these people are very much in love with what they're doing."

The dark-eyed man smiled kindly at her. Was there a tinge of condescension in that smile? Elizabeth had turned away, trying to pay attention to the poetry, though all she could do was think about that smile, that voice, that face.

A young woman had read a poem about taxis in New York. Then there had been a stiff man in tie and cords that read a poem in Japanese and then translated it into English. When Elizabeth glanced behind her shoulder again, the dark-haired man was gone.

She saw him again much later behind a lectern, reading a funny short story. The people in the bookstore were laughing. Of course, why shouldn't they? The story really *was* funny. But somehow the reaction had amazed Elizabeth. The man was reading a short story, and the other young artists in the bookstore, all talented in their own right—well, they were enjoying the reading completely.

After the poetry reading, Rafael introduced himself.

"A few of us are going out for coffee. Do you want to come?"

She had nodded mutely, amazed that a man who could draw laughter and applause from a crowd of strangers would want to have coffee with a beautician.

He drove her to the Miracle Mile in Coral Gables, a beautiful tree-lined avenue of quaint shops and restaurants. When they arrived at the cafe, the writers flocked around Rafael. Everyone in the writing community knew him. They said he had a *real talent*. Rueda had been published already, twice in the *Paris Review* and another time in the *New Yorker*. There was also a local magazine for which he wrote journalistic pieces, but the young writers and poets all cared about the *New Yorker* the most. They seemed so affected by it. Somehow it managed to surface in every conversation.

"Hey Rueda, how does it feel to have been published in the *New Yorker?* . . . It was a wonderful piece, Rueda. It reminded me a bit of that poem you wrote for the *New Yorker* . . . It was just about the time when you wrote that piece that appeared in the *New Yorker* . . ." and so it went.

"Rueda is more successful than most of us will ever be," someone had jauntily confessed that night. Elizabeth had looked at Rafael, trying to match the awe of the writers. They all want to be him, she had thought. They all want to touch him, be part of his success.

Elizabeth hastened her step as she drew closer to the apartment building on Alton Road where she lived. Maybe Rafael had called. Maybe he had left a message for her on her answering machine.

Rafael called Elizabeth two weeks after their first encounter. He took her to the Spanish festival on Ocean Drive, where the Hispanic girls danced *sevillanas* on the sidewalks, twisting their hands and hips and stomping their heels to the frantic thrumming of a Spanish guitar.

Elizabeth envied the Hispanic girls. She wanted to be like

them: elegant and proud and full of history. Rafael smiled at them, his tawny face smooth and brilliant, his eyes sparkling like dark stones set inside soft, golden folds.

"Olé" he shouted and clapped his hands rhythmically, *palmeando*.

Elizabeth had never dated a man like Rafael. Every place they went, someone recognized him, waved at him, shook his hand. He was well read, well dressed, and knowledgeable. He told her he had a talent for understanding people. He could tell about a person just by looking at the expression on his face. He said people gave away clues all the time with their gestures and speech.

"What can you tell about me?" she asked him.

"You're a good person," he said. His face was smooth, relaxed. He fell pensive as he peered at her, but he said nothing more, and Elizabeth was embarrassed to ask him what he was thinking.

The salsa and Latino music and the modern flamenco blared from every other club and bar on Ocean Drive. Hispanic guys and girls knew how to dance to them, shaking their hips and holding their arms up in the sexy swing of the Caribbean dances.

"I want to learn to dance flamenco," Elizabeth said to Rafael, strolling arm in arm with him on the walk, across from the row of the neon-lit Art Deco hotels. Girls were dancing on the beach under the lighted palm trees. They moved in long, sweeping steps, their skirts flaring, their hands curling above their elegantly bent heads.

Rafael's dark, marcelled hair quivered as he laughed. "¡Gringa! That's not flamenco, that's a *sevillana*."

"I'm not a gringa, I am Guatemalteca."

"Come on," Rafael winked.

Elizabeth wrote a postcard to her mother, the first in four and a half years.

Miami is crazy and so much fun. So much diversity here. I speak a little Spanish now, and I've learned to make Ropa Vieja (it's a tasty Cuban dish). Mom, I met a wonderful man. He is Cuban, and he is a writer. I am happy here.

She held the postcard in her hands and stared at it. What was it that she was trying to remember? Eerie how she could hear her heart beat so clear. She squeezed the corner of the postcard. A picture of a long stretch of water lined by pastel-colored buildings . . .

. . . A crowded beach in South Jersey. Dad carrying a folding chair and a cooler, a beach umbrella slung over his shoulder, and an extra six-pack of beer. Mom with the bags with the towels and the suntan lotion. Kids playing paddle. A man throwing a Frisbee to a dog. An obese woman spreading sunblock on her flaccid arms. A little girl screaming as a little boy squirted her with a water gun.

"... must find a corner for ourselves . . ." Dodging between the towels and umbrellas, ". . . look for a little bit of shade."

Had Daddy really said that?

Elizabeth slipped the postcard under her pillow. She pushed the pillow down and held it with both hands.

The *New Times* published an announcement about a writing contest for South Florida residents. The finalists were to read their work in the auditorium on Washington Avenue.

"Congregation of flakes," Rafael declared before he and Elizabeth had even found a seat. Elizabeth spied him quietly, wondering how he could say things like that with such self-assurance. She placed her hand on his and looked at him, but he seemed not to notice. Did he like her? She couldn't say. The few times he had asked to see her he had seemed so casual about it, as though whether she went with him or not really had no importance. She let go of his hand, but still he seemed not to notice.

She listened carefully to the reading. Many of the poems were about homosexual experiences or were tragic, personal accounts of people who suffered with AIDS. To Elizabeth it didn't matter what the poems said. It was the passion that counted, the enthusiasm of the art.

"Thank God it's over," Rafael declared after the last poem was read, a mocking smile curling the side of his mouth.

"Why do you always have to put them down?" Elizabeth asked.

"Most of this stuff is so high-pitched and pretentious. Can't you tell how awful it is?"

"Why is it awful?"

"It's skin-deep."

Elizabeth tried to understand what Rafael meant. Maybe Rafael was just too cocky, she thought. Maybe he was the pretentious one. The writers seemed so talented to her. Even the timid man with the long-sleeved shirts and faded cords who liked to write his poems in Japanese, and the red-haired girl with the faded eyelashes who wrote her poems without punctuation and read them all in one breath, like one long swallow of words.

"Have you brought a poem or short story to read?" someone asked her.

Elizabeth smiled and shook her head. "Not today. But maybe next month."

Rafael laughed, all his white teeth showing.

Elizabeth didn't care that Rafael laughed at all the writers he met. She couldn't understand the things he said about them, and she paid him no mind anyway. It seemed to her that everyone and everything was bursting open with something new, something both dangerous and exciting.

The television news was riddled with accounts of men shooting each other on the highway for petty arguments. The Cuban community was protesting President Clinton's negotiations with Castro, blocking the streets and forcing factories and office buildings to shut down. The rafters—the *balseros,* as the Cubans called them—were floating by the dozens into American waters.

The stories read at the meeting were no longer about AIDS and homosexuality. Many told of desperate people risking property, life, and family for an uncertain dream, the plight of the rafters.

And during a demonstration, a man in a Radio Shack who had just spent $153.00 on a loud speaker asked Elizabeth if she was Cuban. Elizabeth nodded without thinking.

"La comunidad cubana necesita permanecer unida," the man argued excitedly.

Elizabeth wanted to tell the man she didn't speak Spanish, but the man handed her the loudspeaker and beckoned her out of the store. For no reason she could name she followed him, nodding at everything he said.

When he paused, Elizabeth said, "No Castro, no problem." A smile blazed on the little man's face.

Washington Avenue was rowdy with demonstrators. Men, women, children, and old men spilled out of the grocery stores and the Woolworth's and the record store and the Miami Subs. Some of them stood on the street and watched, and others joined the protest, shouting and swinging their fists in the air.

A woman grabbed Elizabeth's arm and asked her something in Spanish.

"No Castro, no problem," Elizabeth said.

The woman shouted, "No Castro, no problem."

"Castro *asesino*," Elizabeth said.

"Castro *asesino*," the woman shouted.

It was hot and dry, and the air was hissing with all the shouts and hoots and the rumbling drums, and the car horns from the traffic were one long howl. Enclosed in a wall of human flesh, Elizabeth thought as the demonstrators pressed around her. She felt protected; she felt safe. And she shouted in Spanish until her throat was sore.

At work on Saturday, when the parlor was full, smelling of hairspray and peroxide and buzzing with simultaneous chatter, Elizabeth told the women that she had gone to the demonstration.

"I was marching on Washington Avenue Thursday," she had said, pushing cotton balls between Mrs. Rodriguez's toes.

"Dat Clinton does no realize, Castro is a pig and a killer . . ."

"Poor *balseros*. Can you imajin dose people? . . ."

The voices of the women rose in pitches. They talked all at once, trying to overcome each other. Elizabeth stared at them, file in hand, mesmerized. She had done this. They had listened to her! She had made the women talk, and now the conversation had taken on a life of its own.

"No Castro, no problem," she said.

"Ay chica, ju're crazy," Maria said, hitting her on the head with a brush.

It occurred to Elizabeth that she could make things happen. She didn't have to stay quiet anymore, listening to the women while she filed their nails. She had a voice too! She had shouted things at the demonstration, and they had listened to her. She had gotten *involved*.

The pictures of the dust-swept patios and the Cuban men in the straw hats playing cards on the beach had started to become real. She thought she could smell the sweat of the men as it mingled with the aroma of the fresh-brewed coffee.

Elizabeth feigned a stomachache and left work early. She bought a *café con leche* at Ana's Mini Market.

"I feel Cuban today," she told Nino.

Nino laughed. "And I feel like Julio Iglesias."

"See you later, Julio," Elizabeth said, paying for her *café con leche*. "Hasta la vista."

She strode hastily toward home, stopping only briefly at Books and Books to buy a notebook and a coffee-table book on the architecture of Cuba. When she got home she glanced at the pictures feverishly, drinking in the brief descriptions typed in small print underneath and to the side. Her hand trembled as she picked up the pen. She stumbled on the opening sentence. She had to write it four different times until she found one she liked.

I remember the Cuban men drinking coffee in their straw hats, it said. She stared at it for a long time, reading it over in her head and then trying it out loud.

"I remember the Cuban men drinking coffee in their straw hats," she said.

Silence in her head. She tried to remember all the things she had heard at the readings: things Rafael had written that she had read firsthand; the translated spurts of the man who wrote Japanese poems; the tricks the red-headed girl used to make her long, unpunctuated phrases sound coherent. Sentence by sentence she crafted her work, reading every paragraph over one hundred times, out loud and in her head. When she finished, she looked at the pages, curling and heavy with ink. She touched them, loving their warm feel under her fingers and the crackling sound they made as she turned them. It was the feel and sound of her work.

"I'm a writer," she said.

The day of the reading Elizabeth felt her hands cold and clammy. The writers stood and read their stories, but she couldn't concentrate on the words. When the people around her laughed, or clapped, or cheered, she winced, startled. She had never felt more disconnected. Who were these people? Where did they come from? What brought them here? She didn't know. She turned to Rafael, and she had the sensation of never having known him either. Suddenly, what one knew and didn't know seemed important to Elizabeth. For instance, it seemed important to her that she didn't know where Dad . . . Jim, she didn't know where Jim was.

Rafael squeezed her hand. "Don't worry," he said. "As long as you don't think you're brilliant, you'll be fine." He winked, his sculpted Hispanic features shifting under the smooth dark skin of his face.

Her hand was sweaty, and she withdrew it.

It was going to be all right, she reassured herself. She glanced over her shoulder at the people around her. Shaved heads, nose rings, and tattoos sitting next to Armani dresses and Kenneth Cole shoes. Yes, she didn't know these people. She didn't know where they came from, but that was all right. They were here. They were, like her, rafters from different oceans, different ways of life. They were all like tiny, shiny pieces of colored glass, gathered together to form a beautiful mosaic. They all fit here. She was where she belonged. It was going to be all right—better than all right! It was going to be terrific.

When her turn came, her heart beat so fiercely that she could almost hear nothing else. Her voice quavered as she hastily introduced herself.

"Elizabeth. I am from . . . Cuba. I am sure a lot of you are, too. Everyone in Miami is Cuban." She paused, expecting laughter—or at least a little drone of amusement.

There was only silence and a slight clinking of coffee cups as the bartenders prepared espresso drinks.

Elizabeth looked into the crowd at Rafael. He shook his head ever so slightly. The possibility of sex with him affected her body like an electric shock. The muscles in her throat tightened.

She straightened herself up, throwing back her shoulders.

"This is my story about how I remember Cuba and about the bloodshed and dictatorship of Castro that has destroyed so many innocent lives."

She smiled. She was sure someone would applaud even if she hadn't read the story yet. These were her people. She understood them. She was one of them, and soon they would recognize she was a piece of the mosaic.

She held the story to her face. "I remember the Cuban men drinking coffee in their straw hats . . ." She paused. Her mouth was dry. The cigarette smoke was hanging like a pall over the patrons of the coffee shop, and she needed a glass of water. She looked for help in the faces of her listeners, but instead she caught sight of a woman only two tables in front of Rafael, smirking and rolling her eyes and whispering something to her girlfriend.

"Like she'd really know shit about Cuba. What an ass."

The girlfriend giggled.

One middle-aged woman smoking a cigarette through a plastic filter glanced back at them and smiled. An impatient boy wearing a T-shirt that said "NIRVANA—WORLD TOUR" lay back in his chair, stretched his long, patched-denim legs, and crossed his arms.

"Come on, man, get it over with . . ." he whispered.

It was odd how suddenly Elizabeth thought she could hear Aunt Lily telling her, "Splendid, dear. Just splendid." It was odd how the longing to hear that voice pinched her like hunger.

"Excuse me, are you going to read?"

Elizabeth turned in the direction of that voice. It was a girl with bleached-blond hair and a nose ring, holding a set of papers in her hands. Elizabeth nodded. The girl nodded also and stepped away.

"I remember the Cuban men drinking coffee in their straw hats . . ." There was feedback on the mike.

"Louder," someone shouted. "We can't hear you."

The written pages rustled in her hands. Where she touched them, the sweat on her fingers smudged the ink. "I remember the Cuban men drinking coffee—" her voice cracked. Her breathing amplified like ugly, supernatural snorts, cracking with the static through the small Peavey amp at her feet.

She looked at her audience again. The red-headed girl with the bleached lashes was whispering something to a young man with a shaved head. The waitress was giving the bartender an order for two cappuccinos. A young, blue-eyed man was complaining about his pie.

"I remember the Cuban men . . ." the red-headed girl cast a quick glance at her, then turned back to her bold friend.

"Louder, please."

"I remember . . . I remember the . . . the Cuban men . . ."

Droning. Coughing. Clinking of glasses.

Elizabeth braced herself and read on, her tongue stumbling on every word, her voice telling the story in a whisper that grew ever softer and faster. The droning rose and rose, and Elizabeth read on, faster and softer, and the conversations in the bar became louder and more mingled.

No one was listening.

She remembered the postcard under the pillow. Slipping in the darkness. The dream she had once of sinking in sand. A phone call and a postcard. And Jim at a bus station. Jim whose face she couldn't remember . . . All that she had missed should have been here. But here there were only strangers.

Elizabeth couldn't finish the story. She held on to her pages in silence. Long moments passed, carried by the casual chatter of the bar. Someone noticed that she had stopped reading and clapped, politely.

"It's all right. It's only stage fright," Rafael said, helping her get up from the stool. "Come on, let's go."

"Where are we going?"

"I'm taking you home."

Throughout the ride Rafael was quiet. She looked at him when he couldn't see her. What was he thinking? What was he thinking!

"Do you want me to come up with you?" he asked, pulling up to the curb across from her apartment building.

Elizabeth stared at the hands in her lap.

"Why was it terrible?" she asked him.

"It wasn't terrible."

"Yes, it was. Tell me why."

Rafael sighed, but he said nothing. His face was smooth and relaxed, his dark eyes gleaming with the refracted light.

"Why was it terrible?"

He shrugged. He looked at the pleats of his pants.

"What if it's going to be like that?" she asked him, looking at the pastel low-rise buildings and the real estate signs sprinkled on the lawns of her block. Sometimes it seemed to her that all of South Beach was for sale.

"What if it's like what?" Rafael asked.

"I thought about it when I was reading, when that woman said I don't know shit about Cuba. I thought for a moment that I was alone. But I mean, really alone. I used to have dreams like that when I was little, you know? That everyone had left the world, and they had forgotten me. And I thought—when I realized that I wasn't going to make anyone believe that I had been to Cuba—well I thought, what if it's like that? What if you can go through an entire lifetime trying to do great things, and no one notices you are there?"

Rafael turned in his seat, his taut, athletic body swinging around to face her.

"And so what, Elizabeth, so what? Why are you so obsessed . . ." His fingers closed on each other like petals of a flower at dusk and touched his forehead. "Why are you so obsessed with being someone different? You think it's exotic to be Cuban? To talk about your relatives who died in some shoot-out, or who are rowing for their lives on a raft somewhere off in the ocean, or coughing up a lung on a cot in Guantánamo? My god, Elizabeth, these things are real. They come up in the newspapers and in conversations in the parlor, but they are real. They aren't just some catchy conversation for the cafeterias in Miami. Someone really knows what it's like to share a chicken with your eight cousins and four sisters and wonder how it's going to get you through next week, or next month, when you get your next chicken. Think about that, Elizabeth. What is the big deal about living your life as a hairdresser? The world needs hairdressers. Otherwise we'd all walk around looking like Hare Krishnas."

"But I want to be like those people, Rafael," Elizabeth cried. "I thought that I could make them listen to me. I thought I really belonged. But I don't belong."

Rafael shook his head, sighed, and looked at Elizabeth as if she were a cute animal in a zoo.

"There is nothing wrong with having aspirations," he said. Elizabeth knew that there was a continuation to the sentence even though it wasn't coming out of his mouth.

"What were you going to say? Tell me."

"Nothing."

"Please, Rafael."

"Nothing, really. What do you want me to say?" Rafael rapped his fingers on the steering wheel. He patted her knee and said, "You'll do better next time."

For a moment they were silent, listening to the zooming traffic, to the rustle of their breaths and sighs. He knew something about her that she wanted—she *needed* to know. But he would never tell her. People always knew things Elizabeth wanted to know. There was some universal password to which she felt she had missed the clue—the password that would allow access to the world of the Cuban women in the parlor, to the world of Rafael Rueda and his train of captive fans.

Elizabeth got out of the car, forgetting to shut the door. She ran up the stairs to her apartment. Her hand shook as she fumbled with the lock. She slammed the door shut behind her and ran to her bedroom and fell face down on her bed.

She wanted to cry and punch the pillow and shout and moan until her throat was sore. It would have been very passionate; it would have been very Latin. But it just wasn't coming out that way.

That Easy
Kind of Life

━━━━━

1

"Who? Who is it?" Max yelled into the phone, unnerved by the salsa blasting from the second floor and the domestic argument it tried to cover up. Pressing the wireless to his ear, Max stared at his tight handwriting on a pad, trying to decipher if five minutes ago he wrote Pfizer or Plasma. He felt hot out here on the porch, beads of sweat sliding between the cuts of his abdominals, but inside it felt even worse, with the AC broken and the fan blowing his papers around.

"Max, it's Dolores," a voice explained at the other end.

Max lipped a silent *fuck*, berating himself for answering the phone in the first place. He grabbed the pack of cigarettes near the laptop and took his time selecting one that wasn't already too damp with the humidity or his own sweat. While he lit up, the wireless wedged between his face and shoulder, Dolores said, "¡Aló! ¡Coño! You there? Max?" Her voice got louder by degrees. Max took a drag of his cigarette and slowly exhaled.

"I hear you," he said.

It was her turn to be quiet. Some static fluttered in his ear.

"I'm at the clinic," Dolores said. "They won't do the abortion unless I have someone here to take me home when it's done."

Max exhaled. The smoke shot out of him in a straight, vigorous whirl, then floated upward, flakes of gray breaking away and slowly fading.

"I can't," he said. "Call your father or your girlfriend or something. If they need to take a taxi, I'll pay for it." He dropped his head back, stretched his legs, and rubbed the tension on the back of his sweaty neck. "I want to finish the survey I'm working on so I can have Ann look it over and polish it up. You know, the girl who works for the *Herald*? She works for me sometimes. I'm dropping the bomb on Sam Davidson about moving to Costa Rica, and I want the survey to look great."

There was silence at the other end. He took a drag of his cigarette and flipped the ashes in the ashtray, and still Dolores said nothing.

"I can't have distractions right now," he said. "I'll give you a call later, OK?"

"It's just a fucking ride, Max," she finally said.

"I'll call later. Promise. Ciao for now, baby." He smacked a kiss into the phone and turned it off quickly. He leaned with his elbows on the table, rubbing the bridge of his nose, his temples, and his eyes so hard he saw bright white spots. He sensed something whirling all around him. He didn't know what it was; he just wanted it to stop. Stop right now, please. Stop and don't come back.

Max bit down on the cigarette with his lips and filled his nose and mouth with the smoke, almost pleased by the way it dried him out from the inside. He wanted to disperse Dolores, breathe her out of his head. She was like exhaust to him, like the crowdedness of South Beach. He used to find her irresistible, talking so tough and looking so sexy, his Dominican salsa princess. Now he couldn't stand the sight of her. It was a stupid mistake. That stupid night. She'd told him she'd just had her period. It was four in the morning, and he was out of condoms. He thought, Just this once.

He heard banging, screeching furniture and something fragile crashing to the floor. Max looked up in the direction of the racket, wishing he could make it stop. Out of control. Everything was out of control, he thought. He wanted out. He was sick of Miami, of his deadlines, of the salsa at all hours, of women expecting things from him, and of the goddamned heat.

Max rubbed his temples and selected Ann's number from the memory dial. His cigarette was almost down to a stub, the smoke winding hotly around his fingers. A female greeting on the answering machine apologized for missing his call in promising, husky tones.

"Hey," Max said without bothering to identify himself. "I could use your help on this survey. If you could drop by this afternoon, I'd really appreciate it. Ciao." Before he could hang up he heard a click, then feedback, then Ann's somewhat breathless voice.

"Max? Hello, Max? Don't hang up."

Max smiled into the phone. The urgency in Ann's voice was a mistake she'd try to make up for, too late, but that was what turned him on about her, that she tried to hold back and couldn't. With some women, sexual attraction was like a sickness. They started out feeling an occasional discomfort expressed in some slip of the mouth or a laughter that rang a bit too enthusiastic; if he teased them long enough, he'd seen that discomfort grow into outright pain. He wondered what the payoff would be of all that restraint with Ann, if it would vindicate itself through the sex when he finally made his move. He tried to think about work again, but all he could think about was Ann, what she would look like with her legs wrapped around his hips.

"Are you still there?" Ann's voice sounded more relaxed. "I just got home. I'm glad you called." She giggled.

"Can you come over?"

"Yeah. Well, I had something to . . . I ran to get the phone and now I can't . . . Oh." Max played with the space bar on the laptop. Finally, she said, "Sorry, I'm so scattered these days."

He felt better already, the tension in his body reduced to a pleasant knottiness in his lower abdomen.

"When?" he said.

"Maybe . . . Well, I have to pick up the dry cleaning . . . Well, then again . . ."

"How about now? I'll be waiting for you," he said, and he clicked off; no chance for no's.

He got up and went inside the apartment. The wall clock hanging over the microwave marked twenty to four. A roach made a slow climb over a sticky note with *Dolores, says important* scribbled hastily over it. He didn't know who wrote it, probably his date from last night. Max grabbed the note, crumpled it and the roach, and tossed them into the garbage can. His fingers flew to the bridge of his nose. On the second floor, a woman screamed, "Te odio. Eres un maldito."

Max went out onto the porch to turn off the laptop and gather his notes. Maybe he shouldn't ask Ann to bail him out again. He still had a couple of hours. It would be like cramming, like back in Thunderbird, where he got his M.B.A. He didn't like asking for favors. Favors were like currency. They had to be traded with care else they'd turn into debts and own him. Still, Ann, she'd helped him before, written up entire sections out of his scribbled notes, polished up his surveys so they looked like he'd spent weeks on them. Ann was a pro. Ann was free. All she wanted was to please him. It didn't get much better than that.

He looked forward to next week, when he'd treat his main client, Sam Davidson, to an expensive dinner, sweeten him with a Cuban cigar, sell him on the Costa Rica idea with a few select words. In Costa Rica Max would get a house with a swimming pool and a live-in maid. He could afford it down there, the economy being what it was. He could have his house in the mountains outside of San José, with a view of the rain forest below, maybe even a glimpse of the smoky green craters of the Irazú. His maid would wash his clothes by hand, hang them out on a rope line to dry in the sun. His shirts would feel a little stiff, but he would smell like the river and the clean air. He would play cards at the village bar at night with the *ticos*. He would tell them anecdotes about the rich America, argue with them over women's breasts, drink home-made wine from thick green glasses that felt heavy in his hands. He'd be the town's main attraction, the newest thing they'd have seen in years. It was that kind of simplicity he wanted, that easy kind of life.

The blasting salsa music was suddenly silenced. A door slammed, and someone in the hallway shouted, You go, girl. Max went into the kitchen and looked into the cabinet, behind the espresso coffee can, behind the bag of granulated sugar, and found a bottle of wine.

2

"Miss? Are you all right?"

Dolores heard the man speaking, but it was only when he touched her that she jolted. "Don't you go touching me!" she warned. Her arm tingled where his finger brushed her. The man looked offended, but he moved away, change jingling in his pocket.

The nurse was looking at her. "We'll get you in in just a moment, OK?" she said from across the hall. Dolores nodded even after the nurse had turned away. She was still seeing the word POSITIVE printed out on the paper with her pregnancy test results, even though that paper was now torn in two and crumpled in the garbage can somewhere in Max's apartment.

"Is *he* with you today?" the nurse had asked when Dolores registered. "You will need someone to take you home after we terminate your pregnancy, you do know that, don't you?" Dolores didn't answer. After awhile the nurse asked, "Do you *know* who *he* is?" but she said it soft and matter-of-fact, like it wasn't meant for Dolores at all.

"My man's coming," she said to no one in particular. The nurse lifted her head, eyed her briefly from behind the reception desk, then scribbled on some form, like she had heard it all before, with that same inflection in the voice, that same pathetic plea.

Dolores was still pressing the receiver of the pay phone between her breasts. She hung up, carefully, as if she were replacing an egg that fell from its nest.

In the waiting room she watched a girl kick her heel against the legs of a vinyl chair. The girl looked too young to be in this place, like she hadn't yet gone through puberty. She stared at Dolores, her prominent brown lips frowning, the whites of her eyes streaked with tiny red lines. There was no *he* sitting next to her, only a white-faced, thin-lipped old woman.

"What you starin' at?" the girl shouted.

When Dolores ran out of the clinic, something had moved up from her chest to her ears and was thrumming in her head, swallowing the sound of traffic, swallowing the words of the nurse who was calling out to her, Miss? Where are you going? The doctor's going to see you in a moment . . . Miss?

The heat was a ball of warmth that engulfed her instantly. It was a force pressing against her, trying to push through the mass of her body.

She walked briskly to the bus stop, her legs moving of their own will. She questioned for a moment the direction she had taken, but too late. She was already too far out on 123rd Street, past the dirty window of the antique shop, past the Cuban cafeteria. She felt too sick for the clinic, something in the way the nurse had said, *We'll get you.* Dolores held her belly with both hands and rubbed it, trying to feel for something. There was nothing. Just her belly. Hard to believe.

A minivan, thickly graffitied with shapely sirens holding up plump breasts, honked as it drove by. A man shouted, *Mamacita.* Dolores pulled down her miniskirt, then her hands returned quickly to her belly, finding it still flat, still usual.

Well, she knew she wasn't Max's only girl. It didn't take much to figure it out, the way he wouldn't take her out on Saturdays, never showed her pictures of his trips, wouldn't let her answer the phone when she was at his place. But why did Max have to mention Ann on a day like this?

At the bus depot there was a smell of rotting fish. The bus let out a harsh hiss as its doors came open. Dolores wanted to throw up. The heat was pressing down on her head, winding about her neck, slithering up the back of her legs. She gulped down the urge to let it all go, this bitter essence, from her guts up through her mouth.

She thought of Max smiling with the side of his mouth, naked, as he was the last time she saw him that way — almost a month ago now. He told her that he was going away, he wanted out of here, he was tired of this crazy ole town. He told her this just after he had fucked her, the taste of him still tart in her mouth.

She gritted her teeth and shivered as if she were cold.

The bus driver said, "You all right, Miss?"

Dolores said, "Transfer, please." She dropped the change into the chute. It was Max. He got to her like that.

"So why you want to go someplace where people's starving?" she had asked him. Max laughed, that's all he did. She heard him in her head now. He was so amused still.

Dolores spotted a seat next to a woman with colored rollers. A waft of urine mixed with a faint scent of rose cologne pervaded her nostrils. She elbowed her way toward the seat. The woman with rollers took a long glance at Dolores and picked up the folds of her nylon print dress, bouncing on her thighs to make space. The nausea came back. Dolores gritted her teeth, gulped it down. She wouldn't throw up here.

The woman said, "Can't be all that bad, girlfriend."

Dolores thought, It was Max's idea, fucking without the condom.

She rested the back of her head against a grimy window. For the first time in years she thought of her mother. A photograph of her with the arch of St. Louis in the background was what came to mind. She couldn't remember much of the picture or her mother's face in it, but the arch was huge and conspicuous, like half a McDonald's sign for space aliens.

They said her mother was in Los Angeles now and married again. Papi said, It don't make a difference where you at. If you stupid and ignorant like *tu madre*, the unemployment line look the same every place you go, but Dolores thought it might be worth it, a life like that, moving on, seeing things. She closed her eyes and tried to picture some of the places Max had been to: Cuba, Panama, and Guatemala. She wondered what the beaches might look like over there and if there were lions in the wild.

Dolores thought, A man like Max will never beat you. You can just tell, his kind of background, the way he talks, like he could teach English to a college kid.

She counted on her fingers the number of stops to the transfer point, then held her belly gentle, like Papi held the shoe box where he kept every lottery ticket he'd ever played and lost. When he wasn't holding it tender like that, his eyes unblinking and focused on nothing, he kept the box stored in the bottom dresser drawer in the bedroom, where Mami used to keep the linen. Every Saturday night, he stared at the TV, his short stubby fingers pressed tightly together, the lottery ticket melting with his hot sweat.

"Papi, losing is free, OK?" she teased him. "You're the only fool paying a buck for it."

Papi stared as if he couldn't hear her, the corner of his eyes more leathery and wrinkled every Saturday. She wondered if he ever thought about St. Louis.

She lied about her age the first time she saw Max. She'd just turned nineteen, but she told him she was twenty-four because he looked older to her. And he was. Almost thirty. They felt the house music pounding, the walls and floor vibrating with the heavy base line. At first Max seemed shy. Smiled a lot. Didn't say much. But when they got going, he left red finger marks on her thighs taking off her panties. Dolores had already been arrested once, but she thought it would be worth it for Max, behind the dance floor like that. It was lucky they didn't get caught. Sometimes the numbers played right.

Max probably didn't believe her that she was twenty-four like she said. He accepted it, though. Later, months later, he said not to worry. He said he'd take care of it if it ever came to that.

Dolores rubbed her belly. The woman in rollers said, "You all right, hon?" Dolores nodded, but something insubstantial that had been moving around inside her froze, suddenly, blocking every word in her throat.

3

When she pulled into the driveway, Ann realized that she had probably run over the cactus again, parking so close to the curb. She shifted into reverse, and this time her right mirror hit the fence and bent so far inward Ann could see the clutter on her car's back seat. The heck with it. She cut off the ignition and checked her makeup in the rearview, smacking her lips and checking for smudges.

Max was out on the porch. He lived on the ground floor, so he must have heard her pull in, she figured. He waved, beckoned her in. He wasn't wearing a shirt.

In her haste she locked her briefcase inside the car. As she fumbled with the keys—was that the trunk key she was trying to jam into the lock?—she noticed that she'd killed the cactus, plowed it down to the ground. She kicked some pebbles over it, a futile attempt to cover up the crime or a symbolic gesture of burial. The thought amused her. Cactus burial.

She was giggling when Max let her in.

He kissed her lightly on the cheek, maybe a bit too close to her mouth. Or was it just wishful thinking? There she went again, wishfully thinking of Max.

She thought of Myra and Ritchie, her two kids in third and first grade, respectively. That's how she managed the businesslike demeanor.

"Have no fear, Captain Ann is here," she joked. No laugh. Oh, God, what a geek she was. "So, when's it due, this time?" she added quickly, dropping the briefcase on the couch, pretending not to notice that the light sheen of sweat on Max's chest was accentuating the cuts and ripples of his well-worked-out upper body. He was lean and well defined, more like a tennis player than a weight-room fanatic. She bent to pick up the couch pillow she knocked to the floor with her briefcase and banged her knee against the coffee table.

"Aw!" she cried, rubbing her sore leg.

He looked up from behind the kitchen counter and observed her without expression.

"I have to fax a draft of it tonight," he said.

Ann realized the table had ripped her pantyhose. Served her right for staring at Max.

"Max, that's not fair," she whined, plopping down on the couch before she could do more damage.

"I'll pay you," he said.

"It's not that . . ."

Max came out of the kitchen holding two glasses and an uncorked bottle of red—it looked like some cheap Chilean wine again, the kind that gave her a hangover headache after only two sips. She shook her head.

"Come on, it will relax you," he said, filling up hers.

"It makes me dizzy, and I can't work."

"We can put off work for a little pleasure, can't we?"

Her hands were shaking a little, so she drank fast. She put down the glass and realized she'd given herself away by drinking so fast. She looked up at Max, who was standing above her, bottle in hand. He held her guilty glance for a second, then laughed and poured her another drink. How did he do that?

"How's Dolores?" she asked him.

"She's fine. Just spoke to her an hour ago."

Max sat in front of her on the love seat. He leaned back and gave himself license to stare at her. It was the kind of thing that scared Ann, the way he could just hold it up like that, not a word spoken, not a crease on his face. That's what made her nervous. Thinking of her kids sometimes helped; thinking of how they cried when Tyler, her ex-husband, had left them; thinking how they looked every birthday that Dad forgot to call. Right now, though, it was herself she saw as a child, a little girl in pumps and miniskirt sitting with a stranger who had offered her candy. But he was no stranger, Max. He was a Tyler; a man she'd been in love with before; a man she took to court, first to tie the knot, then to undo it. And as it often happened when she thought of Tyler, she saw all of the women parade in her mind: Krista, the first, then Silvia, Carmen, Susan, and her *best friend*, Debbie Lee, who fed Myra gummy bears while Tyler *explained*.

"So, what about this deadline?" she asked. "You're going to keep me chained to the laptop all night, are you?"

Max was offering up the kind of crooked smile that made her nervous. "Not to the laptop, no," he said.

She guessed she deserved that. "Well, let me take a look at your thing."

He laughed.

She said, "No, I didn't mean . . . What you got—*wrote*, I mean what you *wrote* . . ." but he kept laughing, that cool, throaty laughter that seemed to travel in invisible waves and tickle her from the inside of her ribs. He sank deeper into the love seat, smiling at her. Had she pleased him? She'd pleased him. Max was just the kind of man you'd want to please, she thought. And wondered why. She never could say, exactly, but it had been the same with her husband, Tyler.

So she flounced a hand at Max and said, "You're terrible," as though she was his mother or aunt and the teasing was only for fun. It was a ritual with them. He tested her and pretended not to notice that she responded. If she made herself too obvious he'd stop, mention something about Dolores or whomever he was sleeping with at the moment. That was how she knew it was a game for him, trying to find out what he could get away with and how much.

She should have used some old-fashioned word to describe him just now, like *incorrigible*, but that might have gotten him started. So she got up and tugged down at her skirt and realized that maybe the shirt she was wearing to match it was cut too low at the neck. Her cleavage was showing. She caught Max staring at her breasts and realized she had been right: the top was cut too low.

"Show me to the laptop," she said with forced panache.

He got up, but he didn't let go of the wine glass. Ann suddenly realized she was feeling hot. Sweat beads were forming on her forehead, for God's sake.

Ann pulled her shirt and blew air with her mouth.

"AC's broken," Max explained. He stepped closer and spoke into her neck when he said, "Or maybe you're driving up the temperature."

"What's with you today? Is Dolores holding back on you?"

The way his jaw set hard against his face, she realized that she'd hit a nerve.

Max smiled broadly and shook his head. Too late, though. She saw him. She didn't quite know what to make of it. There hadn't been a moment like this between them before. They went out to dinner once in awhile. He asked for favors. She obliged.

She said, "You're really serious about this Costa Rica thing, huh?"

He placed the glass on his desk and went for the pack of cigarettes lying behind the laptop, but he went for it with both hands, like it was a life rope in a rafting expedition. She watched him slip out a cigarette and light it, holding it between his teeth. He took a few puffs with eyes closed, and then he opened them again, and they stared right at her, his eyes, right at her pupils. He smiled. Max was Max again.

"Let's take a look at your . . . survey." She turned to the laptop screen, hitting the space bar and the down arrow, doing so several times before she realized the screen was not coming on from power save because the laptop was not turned on.

Max snuffed the cigarette out in the ashtray. As he bent forward, his chest grazed her back. It sent chills up her spine. She hated it when her need was strong like that, making her mind foggy. She didn't want to do it with Max. God, she thought, let me not do it with Max. There was no getting anywhere with him; he was just like Tyler. But who was she kidding? Why was she here? She stiffened, feeling his chest brush against her arm.

"Hey," he said. He was so close to her face it felt like the beach at two in the afternoon without sun block. He took her by the elbow and pulled her to him.

She said, "Hey," and tried to turn back to the laptop.

He slipped his arms around her waist and turned her around to face him. She felt the bulge in his denims press stiffly against her crotch.

"Hey," he said.

She wanted to say, Hey, I'm a single mother with two kids, remember? But the words were blown out from her brain the moment his mouth began to move against hers. And after that, there really wasn't much she could think of saying, except, Come on now then. Let's get it over with.

4

When Dolores turned into the walkway toward the low-rise, she saw him through the window in his den. He was only an indistinct shape, a shadow contrast in the artificial light. She walked slowly up the incline toward his apartment, her belly feeling strangely heavy. Music was playing; she thought she could hear laughter, too. She rounded the gated porch and walked all the way up to the window, cupping her eyes with her hands as she looked in. That's when she saw them, the two of them, cuddling like two cats in heat, frozen in the moment like they were posing for a family portrait at the Porno Emporium. Max was sitting on his desk, giving his back to the window, wearing no shirt. That bitch, Ann-who-works-for-the-*Herald*, was naked on a chair with her legs kicked up, her feet on Max's knees, her big breasts drooping a little on her bony chest.

Dolores backed away slowly from the window and bumped into something hard. It was Ann's car, a white Mazda with one of those rocking window signs announcing Baby on Board. Dolores felt the queasiness in her stomach rising to her throat, and this time she didn't try to stop it. Afterward she felt altogether satisfied to see her vomit splattered all over the hood of Ann's car, even though she'd gotten some on her mouth and on her toes as well. She had a napkin and some tissue paper in her purse, and with that she made herself presentable.

She actually gathered up the courage to bang on the window with her closed fist, gratified by the way the bitch's legs flew up from the desk, her sagging breasts bouncing as she leapt from the chair out of view. Dolores ran to the door and attacked the doorbell.

"Max?" she called out, banging on the screen door. "Open up."

A dog barked furiously at her, his wet black nose sliding between the iron bars of a second-floor balcony.

The door swung open and Max stood before her in his denims, barefoot, shirtless.

"What the fuck do you want?"

He hadn't shouted, really. But it felt like he had. The words, the harshness in them, whipped her across the face. Dolores hit him with her purse, punching him as hard as she could on his shoulders and chest.

"What's that *puta* doing with her tits in your face?" She poked her head in to see Ann crouching way in the back, a shirt wrapped oddly over her breasts. "He's *mine*, you dried-up old whore."

She felt pain in her arm. It was Max gripping her, trying to hold her back. He said, "Shut . . . Hush. Be quiet, now." He pulled her in at first, but as she launched toward the bitch, he tackled her and dragged her back out, his arms holding her in a tight grip.

"Let me get a good shot at that bitch!" she screamed. He shut the door behind him. They were standing on his porch. He settled her before him and let go of her suddenly. She gathered her arms up to her chest and sobbed. Snot came out of her nose. She wiped it with the back of her hand and hid her face in her arms, Max all the while asking, "Dolores? What the hell are you doing here?" His voice was softer in spite of everything.

She looked at his tanned bare feet and said, "What's she doing here?"

"I never said we were exclusive," he said.

She rubbed her eyes, snorted up the tears hanging from her nose. For a while, her sniveling was the only noise. She said, "I didn't get rid of it. I'm going to keep the baby, Max. I want it." She started sobbing again, the words coming out between the jolts of her solar plexus. "I-I-I'm going . . . to . . . keep it. You . . . don't care about . . . nobody . . . All . . . you care about is yourself."

He closed his hands on her arms and jogged her elbows. "You don't know what you're saying."

"No . . . Now you have to . . . take care of me."

"Dolores . . ."

"You said you'd take care of it!" she shouted.

"I gave you money for the abortion."

"You asshole!" she yelled. "It's your baby."

The dog barked, and someone's balcony door slid open.

Max put a hand over her mouth. He didn't press hard, but the gesture provoked her. She smacked his arm so hard it made him step back. He looked across the driveway, then back through the window of his den. She figured he was worried about that bitch Ann.

"It's *your* baby," she yelled. "Don't it mean nothing to you?" It felt like blood vessels had exploded all over her face, like her chest was having its own Fourth of July celebration.

He whispered, "Dolores, I told you I'm moving *away*."

"You're not going nowhere." She tried to slap his head. When he dodged to miss her, she punched him in the chest.

Max held her by the wrists but not as gentle as before. "You're acting like a spoiled little girl."

She yelled, "You can't go. I'm pregnant, don't you get it?" He dug his fingers so deep into her wrists that she squealed, "Oh God, you're hurting me. You're hurting the baby."

Instantly he let go of her. He was white in the face, mouth slightly ajar, eyes glassy and alert. He looked so surprised, like it was the first time, maybe, that he ever thought about it, the baby being in there. Dolores put a hand to her belly, eyes dropping there a moment, then fixing back on him. He looked so different suddenly. Like Papi in some way, when he held up his shoebox with the lottery tickets. It made her sick to see him like that.

She said, "You really going? You walking out on me and my baby?"

He stood so perfectly still that she thought he might not even be breathing. Then stiffly he said, "I don't want your baby."

"Don't tell me that," she shouted. "You should of told me that before you came inside me." She moved to slap him, but he stepped back, so frail he looked, like she might break him. She said, "You chicken shit. You go acting like the big man in town, macho shit, fucking your woman without no rubber, and now you're just a chicken shit."

"Ssshhh . . ." He hissed. He opened his mouth and sucked in some breath, the muscles in his stomach bunching up like he was about to shout. But he just gaped. Finally he said, "Look, it was a mistake. I didn't think this would happen. I couldn't find a condom, and I just wanted to . . ." He rubbed his neck, looking away. "I didn't think it would happen," he repeated.

"Is that all you got to say to me? You just give me some cash and walk out like I don't exist? You make me sick!" she spat. "You just don't care about nothing. You so in love with yourself, you can't love nobody else. There's no room in that little heart for me and this baby."

She realized that she'd said it for him. There was something in his silence that lingered there, affirming what she'd said. It felt a little like breaking a spell. All that held her up from the clinic to this place, all the wishing that had her captive since she first saw him with the part on his hair so straight and his smile so quick and wicked, was gone, just like that.

She said, "You go on to your bitch in there. Me and my baby don't need you, anyhow."

She turned on her heels, holding her head up high, flaunting the hippy walk that got him interested in her in the first place. For a second or two she half expected him to call out after her, to wobble barefoot over the gravel and beg for her to reconsider, but when she turned into the street and still he had done nothing to stop her, it was as if she'd found her way out of Wonderland, everything finally looking the way it actually was.

5

Max's hand folded around the bar of the iron gate closing off his porch. He shut the gate and swallowed the stale taste of tobacco in his mouth. A man shouted at the dog to shut up. It was the man upstairs, the one in the argument that morning.

"Can't get no peace around here," the man shouted. The dog kept barking.

Sweat was dripping from Max's hair down his cheekbones. Dampness clung to his jeans. Inside a waft from the fan attacked him with warm air. He shrugged at Ann.

"Hot," he said as he sat on the couch, his eyes on his own hands. Finally, he lit himself a cigarette. The ashtray was full and heaped with ashes. He busied himself emptying it in the garbage; then rinsed it clean in the sink, Ann watching him quietly all the while. He let the water run. He ran a hand through his hair and noticed he'd been running his hand through his hair too much.

Ann said, "I have to pick up the kids from the baby-sitter."

Max turned back to the coffee table. He needed something to hold with his hands, so he sorted through his business and scuba magazines. He made a big stack of them and packed it hard on the floor. A long curl of ashes dangled from the tip of his cigarette. He drew on it anyway. The ashes fell on his jeans and rolled to the floor still in a tubular shape. He wanted to say, Ann, I just can't help it.

But he said, "Fuck."

And Ann said, "OK, Max. I'm really going."

Then it came out of him, a suppressed whine oozing out unwillingly. He said, "Listen, I'll pay you for your trouble. I really need this job done." He was on his hands and knees stashing the magazines under the coffee table. He stood up, brushed his hands free of dirt particles, and tried to smile up at Ann, the eyelids drawn to tiny cracks.

She said, "You can't expect me to bail you out every time." Her face jerked to the side as if he'd slapped her with his looks. "I really can't stay." When she looked at him again her eyes were glassy.

He held his cigarette to his lips between his thumb and forefinger. He drew on it, looking at her through the curling smoke. He guessed she must have been in her mid thirties. He had never slept with someone her age before, though he himself was almost thirty. In bed he saw a scar below her pubic hairline, an ugly white heirloom of a C-section. He'd let his fingers run the length of it slowly, her skin smoothing to his touch. Thinking this made him feel better.

"Why don't you just relax a little," he said, lacing a finger through her hair.

She crossed her arms, holding her purse in front of her like a schoolteacher. The skin was smooth on her face, tight on her cheekbones, soft around the mouth. Her hand brushed his bare arm as she slinked past him. It felt sensitive where she touched him, tingly where he had held her hair. He thought she'd say something when she picked up the briefcase from the couch, but she just smiled at him, a hand lowering gently on his shoulder and lifting again.

6

Ann saw her weeks later: Dolores, waiting at the bus stop, a thin silhouette wavering with the heat rising from the pavement. It was two days since Max had his number disconnected, and Ann thought, What the heck.

She had to honk several times before Dolores lifted her head from the magazine, her large brown eyes staring uncertainly. Ann honked again.

"Come on," she shouted, releasing the door lock from the control panel.

Dolores stepped off the curb. When she got in the car, she turned her head to the back seat, where Myra had just climbed over and Ritchie was strapped in a car seat. Dolores's lips stretched over her gums.

She said, "Well, hello there, you two."

Myra said, "Hello." Ritchie stared, his pudgy hand pulling down his lower lip.

"Where to?" Ann asked, pulling away from the curb. She turned to Dolores when she stopped at a red light at the main intersection and still had gotten no answer.

Dolores had both hands covering her mouth, her eyebrows turned up. The magazine that spread open on her lap announced, "Ten Ways to Tell if Your Man Is Cheating." The squeak that came out of Dolores was a giggle. Ann started giggling, too.

"He still around?"

Ann shook her head. The light turned green, so she stepped on the gas pedal, not thinking, just driving. "Some men are insecure like that." Then she said, "I'm sorry. Really."

Dolores curled the magazine in her hand and let the pages scroll through her fingers.

"You got a cigarette?" she asked suddenly.

Ann shook her head, nodding to her kids in the back.

"Them yours? How old?" Dolores asked. There was a nervous energy to her that made Ann realize just how young she was. Another red light.

"I don't know where Max went," Ann said.

"Costa Rica. He told me he was going to Costa Rica."

"That's a whole country." Ann tapped her fingers on the steering wheel. "Max closed down the business. He lost the contract with Sam Davidson, and Sam was keeping Max afloat. That last survey did it, the night you threw up on my car." She stared at Dolores, waiting for an apology, but none came.

Dolores looked at her long nails, acrylics of the American flag. It was hard to say how much of this mattered to her, if she cared about anything or anyone. Like Max.

"I got it done, you know," Dolores said. "Last week."

"What?"

Dolores's thumbs laced together; her hands rested on her belly, then fluttered up like birds in flight. "The baby," she said. She sucked in her stomach, showing off its flatness.

Someone honked. Ann jolted. The light had turned green. She was stunned a moment by the news, the uncertainty of her own reactions, then she stepped lightly on the gas pedal. On the sidewalk, orthodox worshipers trickled out of a Hasidic temple, the women with long skirts and shawls over their heads, the men in long black jackets and tall hats. The image stayed with her a moment before it was overtaken by the sight of golf courses, waterways, and golden palms. She had a feeling in her stomach like something was moving inside, alien and yet still a part of her.

Dolores said, "Don't you go feeling bad for him, now. Don't feel bad for him, none. The man was ready to walk out on his own baby. He don't care."

Ann took a glimpse of her own kids in the back seat. What could she say about it, really? This was not her story. This was not about her at all.

"You're not telling Max I got rid of it, are you?" Dolores asked. The pitch in her voice dropped almost an octave. She waited for a response with her lids half lowered.

"Dolores, I don't know where Max is."

"But if he calls, you're not telling him, are you?"

Ann sighed. Ritchie had fallen asleep in the back seat, and Myra was looking out the window with her finger stuck in her mouth. The world catches you unprepared, she wanted to tell them. She should have said it to Max. She should have said *something*, anyway. But she just shook her head. She shook her head no, and Dolores giggled.

7

Max had his laptop and all his belongings packed tight in a knapsack slung over his back. There was no one waiting for him at the airport in San José. He had no place to go. Large fans hung from steel transoms on the ceiling, and men in green uniforms walked busily around, checking tickets and passports, herding tourists and homecoming passengers to the correct waiting lines.

"Gringo," he joked, showing the Aduana officer his passport.

The officer was unsmiling as he pointed at the knapsack. "Saque lo qué tiene."

A group of stewardesses sailed past him and smiled down at the socks, underwear and shirts, jeans, and sneakers that Max lined up on the counter. He had sold all that he owned, which wasn't much in the first place. What he couldn't sell he had given away. The money that he made from what he sold and most of what he had in the bank he sent to Dolores in a check, in an envelope with no return address. The child would be all right, he told himself. The stewardesses smiled at Max; they giggled together. Max stared at their buttocks jiggling through their tight skirts.

Outside the terminal he caught a bus to take him to the city center. He didn't know where he'd sleep, but somehow he knew he'd be all right. In the end, he was always all right.

A crumbling poster on a crumbling building announced the lush wilderness of the Braulo Carillo National Park. A chairlift was shown hanging from a thin wire above the tangled tree canopy. Just below it hung a sign announcing two kilometers to the nearest McDonald's. The air was thick with exhaust from the stationary buses, taxis, mopeds, and cars. The paved streets milled with people: workers from the travel agencies, tourists arriving and departing, *tícos* working and living in the neighboring area.

On the bus, Max placed his belongings on an aisle seat in the back and took the window seat for himself. He felt suddenly exhausted. He rested his head against a grimy window and closed his eyes. He was startled by a knock.

"Señor, ¿quiére comprar unos billetes para una gira al volcán?" It was a young boy trying to sell him tickets to a tour. Max shook his head. The young *tíco* held the ticket up to his window and smiled, revealing huge gaps between his small white teeth.

Max said, "No," but he said it softly, something in his throat failing. He slid the window open a crack, searching his pocket for a cigarette, telling the boy, "No quiero. No quiero nada."

Hugo,
Arthur,
and Bobby Joe

I'm living with Bobby Joe now. It's not the best thing in the world, but he wants to marry me. He talks about it all the time, as if it were a sure thing, talks about mortgages, car loans, maternity coverage on our health insurance. Lately, when he talks about it, I just shut up. The times I told him I wasn't sure if marriage was what I wanted, he went stiff like cardboard. You're thirty years old, he shouts. You'd better start deciding what you want. I get intimidated by shouting, so I say nothing, and I lie on the futon in the guest room looking at the cracks in the paint and the grease spots on the wall, wondering what life would be like without Bobby Joe.

I've been with Bobby Joe for three years. I met him right after Hugo broke up with me, and back then I thought, This is what I need, this Bobby Joe. I felt somehow I needed to be protected, walled in. Safe from Hugo. Safe from his late night phone calls, his menthol breath, his bed confessions.

I still see Hugo in my dreams sometimes. It's usually something about him disappearing through a crowd or in a great big building full of people and me not being able to catch up to him. I'm one of those people whose dreams are like life. I hear him breathing. I touch the sweat on his brow. I hear my own footsteps and feel the pebbles and stones under my feet. When I wake up I smell Hugo on me, a faint blend of cigarettes, cologne, and clean sweat. Then I'm afraid to let Bobby Joe get too close to me before I take a shower.

Things are OK, now. They are steady, predictable. I have a good crowd of friends. I have a good time. My girlfriends like Bobby Joe. It makes things easy.

Steady relationships. It's like taking a slow boat through the intercoastals, where the manatees swim. After three years of Bobby Joe following me into the bathroom, asking me, What are you doing? (what does one do in the bathroom?), it feels like I crossed the channel, finally, like I stand on solid ground.

I can take this attitude when my friends call, feeling like Jesus in the desert. Emma, for instance: she sounds breathless on the phone. She tells me, I met someone. He's a *photographer*, freelance, worked with all the big ones, *Condé Nast, National* . . . His name is Arthur, but he likes to be called Ace. You *have* to meet Ace. You and Bobby Joe would just *love* Ace.

Everything dangerous starts out as a joke.

I tell her, Ace? Emma, he's pulling your leg!

Freelance photographer. There is a kind of lure that comes with that profession. Ace—Arthur—wears it out for all it's worth. He's not around very often, but when he is, he's sure to be surrounded by some handsome crowd of slick, fashionable people looking like they've just leaped out of some full spread for *Vogue*. All that moving around. All that traveling. Can't figure out where Ace meets these people. Where do they come from? I picture Arthur ordering friends and party guests through some Internet catalog, the way busy executives order wives from Thailand.

Arthur's good with the crowds. Looks like he belongs right there in the middle of all that's happening, a peevish kind of smile on his lips as he shrugs and says he's photographed just about every corner of this world. I try to keep in mind that silly Ace stuff, but he stuffs a hand in his khakis, leans a bit against the wall, says if he's missed a place, it's likely it wasn't worth seeing. He looks straight into my eyes as he says it, the smile hanging soft on his lips, the voice flowing smooth from the side of his mouth, like the smoke of his cigarette, and I have no doubt that when he says it, it's absolutely true.

Arthur shows up to every place with a different girl. If I ask him about this or that woman he was with the other night, he smiles, shrugs a little, his eyes looking above my head or at the center of my forehead, like he honestly doesn't know who I'm talking about. He changes the subject, mentions the time he dove in a shark cage in Australia, when he ran with the bulls in Pamplona, or when he got harassed by soldiers while hunting in Zambia. More than once he talks about his scuba excursions—the difficult stuff, like wrecks and night dives. And do I know that the wrecks and night dives are considered the hard-core, difficult stuff?

Arthur's pad is not much of a luxury place. A living room with a pull-down and a bedroom stuffed floor to ceiling with boards, tripods, lenses, viewers, and boxes upon boxes with slides of his shots. On one of the walls in the living room there is a poster of a matador advertising a bullfight in Mexico and, adjacent to that, one of his original shots; a surfer catching a Hawaiian wave that turned out as cover for an issue of *Islands*.

Arthur hits a button on the answering machine and keeps talking about his latest shoot, but all we hear are these sticky female voices coming out of his machine: Ace, please, come on over. Oh, Arthur, please call tonight. There's this great party, Ace, please. Please call at five, we'll go work out together. At seven thirty, a movie. I'll answer my phone till eleven. It's OK to call after midnight. Please call. Please.

Bobby Joe is laughing that wink-wink, male-bonding stuff, acts like if he rubs elbows enough, some of that Ace stuff will stick to him. For a while I keep it to myself, but the word just keeps coming up. Please, Arthur. Please. Please call me. Please don't forget. Please.

Finally, I have to say it: I've never begged a guy like that.

Arthur gives me this smile, like, Don't kid yourself.

———

Women who beg disgust me. I see them walk up to a guy, slip an arm around his waist, smile the kind of smile that promises something, and walk off with him somewhere dark and quiet. I think about it. How do they do that? What do they say? It all seems so easy with them. They make off with the Arthurs and the Hugos, take them places I can't follow, those crowded buildings in my dreams . . .

———

I think about Hugo too much. I think about him when I'm not even thinking at all. A quiet, soft-spoken man, moving along apologetically as if he were embarrassed by his good looks. I think about his eyes. Hematite dark. Always seemed to attract a flicker of light, even in the most intimate darkness. I looked at those eyes a long time. Like his essence was there, and the rest of him, his body, his face, his words—just accidental. I trusted the eyes more than the words. It was the source of my confusion. I still try to figure it out. I'm still grasping at memories of his words for clues. Hugo. I just couldn't hold on.

For months Arthur turns up at our place unexpectedly. I make breakfast on Saturday, and he shows up just as Bobby Joe and I are sitting down to eat. I come home a little late from the office, and there he is, drinking with Bobby Joe. He gets up and strides toward me with his hand out, as if I were the most important person he's seen all day.

Things get predictable. He calls every day, and if I pick up the phone, he's sure to make an effort to start a conversation: he asks me about my job, cracks a joke, tells me an anecdote about his latest trip. Anything to keep me on the line. Whenever he can slip it in, he uses words like *orgasmic* to mean nice, or *let's get naked* to mean he feels high on life. He kisses me on the cheek by way of greeting, each time closer to the mouth, holding my face to make sure I won't turn away or taking the time to run a hand through my hair.

Then he stops that. Just when I start expecting him to do things like that, Arthur stops. When I talk to him, he looks distracted, something else on his mind, and if he answers me, it's with a kind of annoyance in his voice, his eyes flicking around the room, looking for a different face. I see him at parties glued to some new girl, usually someone young and flippy-looking, wearing the latest spandex fashions. If I come close to him or surprise him alone in a quiet corner, he says, So where'd you lose your Bobby Joe?

I thought I had Arthur figured out. When I realized I didn't is when I started to get interested.

Hugo used to say I was a good listener. He said my eyes told him I cared. He talked quietly and slowly about his divorce, about how alone he felt when he left Brussels to come to Miami. He felt so desperate when he got here that he walked right into a problem on his very first day, a knife scar on his left arm and no wallet for his trouble. His face would scrunch up as he talked to me, his eyes become glittery and very serious. I thought he didn't know he was on the verge of tears, and I held my breath, thinking that I could stop him from crying.

All I want now is a friend, he'd said, his dark stare cutting into mine.

Friend. I thought it meant I was something.

I have a confession to make, Olga says.

My hands curl around the receiver, I wrap the phone cord around my waist. Olga, I mouth to Bobby Joe. Bobby Joe has to lean on my shoulder, press his ear against mine. He needs to hear Olga's voice. I don't know if Bobby Joe thinks I lie to him. Sometimes I think he senses Hugo, the essence of him, standing like a ghost in the bedroom, watching us both.

Olga sounds apologetic.

She says, Arthur and I . . . Well, you know.

Something electric goes through me, like I rubbed a wool sweater on a windy day.

Our Arthur?

She goes on talking about it. Dinner at a Vietnamese restaurant, drinks at his place, the promise of a weekend in Bermuda.

Sometime after the first few minutes I stop listening. My tongue is rubbing against the back of my teeth. There's that taste again in my mouth, like licking a piece of cold metal.

I'm sensing Hugo right now. He's standing in this bedroom by the lacquered Formica chest of drawers that Bobby Joe picked out from the Sears catalog last year; Hugo, standing with his arms folded, a glitter from the night lamp in his dark eyes; Hugo, watching Bobby Joe watching me listening to Olga talking about Arthur. He's smiling, I imagine, Hugo is. Smiling sensitively and cautiously even, amused by the secrets I'm hearing.

Hugo liked to purge his guilt with truth. He'd sit on the bed and sigh a little, his eyes holding on to me, cradling me in some infinitely gentle, hematite space. I have a confession to make, he'd say. It was always someone I didn't know. But he'd never say, That girl, that woman, that intern at the office. It was Nancy, Stacey,

Marianne. Names. Identities. Women he'd describe in painful detail. He'd fill up with air when he'd finished talking, then grab me, hook me in a tight, endless hug. His kisses would fall along the side of my face, over my ears, and on the back of my neck. I'm sorry, he'd say.

And later, when we were naked again, he'd whisper, If I look into myself, I'll find you. You are the mirror of my soul. It scares me to look there. I'm afraid of what I see.

I don't know why, back then, I thought he meant he was in love with me.

When I first moved in with Bobby Joe, some days I'd still wake up with that taste. I'd go to the bathroom and try to make myself throw up. Or I'd stand in the shower and cry, quietly, dryly, like it wasn't even worth the tears. Like the fact that I'd known all along about Hugo's women discounted my hurt.

———

So I learned something. With Hugo it was about love, about the untruth of love. With Arthur it's about pride. It's about retaliation. The dialogue is open in the silence. We share a glance, a fleeting touch, a smile in the right moment. The women turn up and over, and I feel the invisible slap, the quiet insult. Why them? Why not me?

Emma talks a mile a minute when she finally decides to tell me about Ace. Her voice keeps speeding up, afraid I'll interrupt. Or maybe she's afraid I won't. Silence: the bell of judgment.

Emma's hands are twined over the damp stone table. We sit in the back of the cafe near my place, in the garden area. We sip our cappuccinos with skim milk, nibble at our almond biscotti. I notice her body, so still in contrast to the rushing of her words. Only her eyebrows move. They go up and down. Sometimes the folds near her eyes crinkle. She looks like she hasn't slept in days. Emma, with her buttoned-up sweaters, the schoolgirl skirts, the pink hair clips. Who would have guessed?

I think of Arthur. Him and that low, slanted stare, the blowing of the smoke from the side of his mouth, the smile that creeps up sideways on his face when I'm not watching, not paying enough attention.

Emma breathes over her coffee, runs her fingers through her hair, rubs her eyes.

Oh God, she says through her hands. Olga will kill me.

I'd like to tell Emma I know how it feels. It's not as if I've never lived. The first time, it's happiness all over. Happiness like a damp cloth on your skin. Later the doubt comes. Later is when the grieving starts.

Jane thinks she sees something the rest of us can't. I hear it in her voice when she talks about Arthur. She thinks it will be different with her.

She says, I don't know why Emma would be upset. They were *never* something official.

She sits across from me at the News Cafe, our sidewalk table vulnerable to pedestrian traffic and to the restrained and contrived writhing and sidling of waiters in red aprons. Her fingers trace the hickey on her neck. She flicks the cigarette ashes to the ground, sporting her confidence like the tight cut-off beach top she would never let her daughter wear.

She says, Poor Emma, she wanted to define. Like he *owed* her anything. Anyway, it's not like I'm runner-up.

Jane inhales. She takes it all in, the exhaust from the revving Harley about to pull out from its valet space, the smell of omelette with jalapeños and salad with vinaigrette, the menthol and low-tar cigarette smoke, the scent of Arthur's cologne, probably still impregnated in her skin, her clothes, her olfactory memory. She sucks it all up with that one breath, swallows it along with the last words. Then, she exhales.

I listen to the cups clinking as the waiter cleans our table. I hear the forks and knives clashing together, metal on metal.

I made the mistake of telling Bobby Joe about Hugo once. Bobby Joe wanted to know everything, details that felt like stones in my stomach, like the size of his penis, or the color of the panties I wore the times we'd made love. Bobby Joe would get all stiff and silent as I talked. When I tried to put my arms around him he'd just pull back and ask me more questions.

Did you swallow? Did you use condoms or were you on the Pill?

When I didn't answer, I could see the thing growing in his head, eating away at his thoughts. I listened to myself giving him the details. I listened to it all over again. And Bobby Joe, who is an atheist, went to church afterward and prayed to Mary and the child not to make him jealous. Bobby Joe: the devil and the saint.

——— ———

Arthur's with a Japanese girl. She's sweet as grape jelly and not much more interesting than that. I want to tell Arthur he shouldn't date nice girls. Nice girls are easy to break.

It's Jane's party when we first see the nice girl. Jane pulls me to the side, her fist against her teeth.

Who the hell is *she*? How *old* do you think she is? Nine*teen*? Twenty?

Later, scotch and water on her breath, she shrugs it off, says, Why not? It's all right, really.

Some women think they have it down; they think they know the art. I think something always sticks to us, like grease or a bad smell. The more the flies come near, the more we look like trash.

——— ———

Hugo liked to play a game. We looked at each other in silence in a place full of people, like an auditorium or a restaurant. I'd always be the one to break it off first. I'd get red and start to giggle, or I'd say something awkward like, People must think we're strange. Let them, Hugo would say, unflinching, his stare boring into mine, his eyes so dark. The light struck against them, so I could see myself, a tiny, blurry shadow inside them.

There is always a game to be mastered, always a lesson to be learned. With Bobby Joe it is the game of lies. The lesson is that honesty is overrated. My past is my own.

The game I never learned with Hugo required nerves of steel. If I wanted to keep him, I had to pretend that nothing he did mattered, not the absences of days, not the certainty of his cheating, not the sexual scents of other women he'd bring into our bed when we made love. He wanted me to be sure of me for the two of us. But I wasn't sure of me.

I nearly lost it in the end. I waited for him on the steps of his apartment building. I'd hide in the mailbox room when he walked in with his new lovers. I waited until I saw the women come out again, alone, without lipstick, their hair messy, their mouths smiling.

Later, I learned to seal myself off, shut my feelings in, airtight.

I tell myself I've learned Arthur's game quite well. I know how to sit next to him without looking obvious, I know the game of accidental contact, brush my knee against his, pull away if he shows that he noticed. I am chatty and lively whenever he is within earshot. I am careful about things he cares about, like fashion, and posture, and the way I dance. I will speak to all of his friends and be warm and very charming, but I will barely smile at him, and then only when I catch him staring at me.

Sometimes I say to myself, I'm winning.

I change my strategy to keep him guessing. For weeks I don't call him, or I'll avoid his presence in company. When he calls and I pick up, I hand the phone to Bobby Joe. I can hear the frustration in Arthur's voice when I cut him off. So did you want to speak with Bobby Joe? I say. Sometimes he breaks down. He says, Hell no, I want to speak with you.

He knows how to get even with me.

While he watches the basketball game with Bobby Joe, he says his new girlfriend from Australia will be coming to stay with him for a while, maybe even a few months. I put on my tights and my tank top and pace around the living room, pretending to look for my sneakers. I have been working out with a trainer for a year. My body is lean, toned, and sculpted. I bend over when I find the sneakers, my tight round butt propped up and in full view. I see Arthur through the reflection in the french doors, looking at me, his neck barely straining.

I'm going to the gym, I say, wrapping a sweatshirt around my waist. I give Bobby Joe a wet kiss. That's for the girlfriend from Australia.

I know men like Arthur. I know them. I am afraid of them. I can't ignore them. I fight them like some warped, sci-fi Joan of Arc, but I'm inevitably drawn to them even as I'm terrified of them. Eve lured by the forbidden fruit. A desire stronger than the promise of eternal peace. Maybe I just keep looking for clues. Maybe I think they hold the answer to all I didn't know, could never know about Hugo.

It's booming inside Arthur's Jeep, with the rain pelting at the fabric top, the wind clawing at the plastic windows like it wants to come in. He's taking me home from the Japanese girl's house, where we just had lunch. Bobby Joe's at the office, working the weekend to prepare himself for an expo where his company will exhibit next week. He doesn't mind that I have lunch with Kyoko and Arthur. I wonder sometimes why Bobby Joe trusts me with Arthur when he won't trust me on the phone with Olga. I wonder why he can't sense it with me the way I used to sense it with Hugo, when the freezing sets in inside, when no sex, no kindness, no expensive dinner out is enough to hold us together anymore.

In the Jeep, while he drives, Arthur says, Kyoko's not my lover. I don't know why anyone would say a thing like that. And I've never slept with Jane, or Olga, or Emma, for that matter. You imagine all this stuff. You think I'm some sort of gigolo.

I want to laugh in his face. I want to hurt him for having used them before me, for leaving me behind and then lying about it. I am forcing my hands relaxed, I am forcing my mouth to smile. Play the game, I tell myself. Nothing matters.

What is it exactly that you are trying to do? I ask. Trying to clean up your act for your exotic girlfriend in Australia? I hear wedding bells, Arthur.

Sooner for you than for me, he says.

Shows how little you know me, I say.

He steps on the brakes, slowly, and turns his head to find my eyes.

Well, maybe we should fix that, he says.

He pulls off to the side and onto the grass. He cuts the engine off, and his arm wraps tightly around my shoulders.

What the hell are you doing? I ask, but there's no answer from him. His mouth is so close to mine, I can see every detail. I've thought about that mouth so much. I close my eyes and see that mouth, see it even as I feel it pressing against mine, see it as Arthur's cold hands touch my body so that I begin to moan.

I have this need for Bobby Joe to protect me from men like Arthur, men who stay around only as long as I will play the game, only as long as that game is interesting. I curl up next to Bobby Joe on the couch. We are watching a Holocaust movie and I'm crying. I have been crying steadily since this afternoon. Bobby Joe's found a reception hall he likes. For our wedding. When the caterer shook my hand earlier this afternoon I tasted it again, cold steel on my tongue.

Bobby Joe's voice is very gentle as he rubs my feet, as if he senses it, the distance coming between us. He is careful now to ask me where I've been, or why Arthur left a message for me, or why I have worked so late at the office.

What's wrong, he asks from time to time.

It's the movie, I say.

Bobby Joe rubs my feet as I cry. He says, We don't have to do it if you're not sure. We can wait a little longer. Something in his voice is like the girls saying please from inside the answering machine at Arthur's house. Please. Please.

I want to tell Bobby Joe that I want this. I want the wedding, the house, the kids, the forever plans. But there is no anchor here for me, only ropes that drag me down. I want Bobby Joe to hold on to me. I want him to keep me from drowning. But I can't open up my mouth, because the only words in there right now are Hugo, oh my God, oh, Arthur, please.

Turn
These Stones
into Bread

1

"So, what do you say?" Aaron said on the phone to his father, who was still silent, musing the question. He wondered what his father understood about this invitation to go hiking together, if he thought it was a challenge, or a gift, or what.

"How long did you say you wanted us to be out there?" his father asked.

"Just a few days."

"Did you have a particular place in mind?"

"Does that mean you want to go?" asked Aaron.

His father let out a sigh so deep that static fluttered in Aaron's ear. Aaron was tempted to hang up. They had never spent any time together that hadn't either been prescribed by a court of law or requested by his mother, and now he couldn't imagine why he ever thought going on vacation together would be a good idea. His plan finally seemed childish. He wanted to call his shrink and call the whole thing off, tell her what a stupid idea it all had been, but what would Dr. Piper say to him if he turned back now?

"Why are you still so angry at your father?" Dr. Piper had finally asked him yesterday, culminating three months of therapy on the subject of his father. Her thin, frail body had bent in two, her torso leaning forward, as though Aaron's pent-up frustrations were her frustrations as well. "He was unhappy in the marriage. What did you want him to do?"

"He didn't honor my mother. He violated the sanctity of their marriage for some . . . some whore!"

"And you think they should have stayed together, even though he was unhappy?"

"Yes!"

"Would you?" she asked, her pen suspended above his file. "Would you stay in an unhappy relationship, knowing that you didn't love your wife anymore?"

"He had children. He had me. I was only two years old, for god's sake."

"So, you're angry that he abandoned *you*, not that he abandoned your mother."

Aaron had stood up and pointed at her, feeling like she'd stolen something. He wanted to surprise her with an answer that would scramble all the intellectual patterns of that university-acquired logic in her mind, but he could think of nothing clever enough, so he clenched his teeth and said, "Yes. I guess so. Yes." Then he sat, weary, as if admitting to that more-than-obvious claim had punctured his lungs, and air was leaking out of him slowly. Dr. Piper had her pen in her mouth, looking at him with that look that scared him, as though she could see the course of his blood through every vessel and vein in his face. He thought she could read his mind.

He had never forgiven his father for walking out on the family, but to that moment he had always thought of his father's act as the cause for collective suffering, a catastrophe that hadn't so much happened to *him* as much as something that had been aimed at the structure of the world he lived in, affecting in equal shares all who had been a part of it. It was impossible to talk about what his father had done without considering his mother, the years she worked two jobs, the winter she took them to Quebec to live with their grandparents when Aaron and his older brother, Garret, had to learn French and were teased by the Canadian children for their American accent. At home, the disaster had almost become part of their bread and wine at dinner, their milk and cereal at breakfast. *Father walking out.* It was the reason for the bad public school Aaron and Garret had to attend, the reason for Mom having no patience and yelling at everything they did, and for Garret having his nose broken in the ninth grade. But the abandonment had never been anything so wholly his until Dr. Piper had said it, until she had spat it out for him in that simple, matter-of-fact statement: abandoned *you.*

Abandoned *me.*

Those words . . . they were notes he could sound in the hollows that existed between the memories of his dad and the fantasies he had contrived to make up for his absence.

"I don't know," his father said on the phone. "It's not that I don't want to spend time with you, but I'd have to take more vacation time than I'd planned."

Aaron fingered a Michael Jordan pin that he kept in the drawer of his office desk. There had been a life-size poster of Michael Jordan in his and his brother Garret's room when they were children, and Aaron remembered staring at the poster, imagining that he'd come back from school one day to find Michael Jordan sitting at the wicker table on the porch, having hot chocolate with his mother. Jordan would get up from his chair, always in full team getup, the red shirt with the Bulls horns, the smile on his face like the Cheshire cat's, and his humongous hands swinging at his sides as he strode toward Aaron. One of those hands would touch him on the shoulder, and Jordan would peer down at him and say, "Your mother and I decided I should adopt you."

He'd told that story to Dr. Piper, and she had said, "Why haven't you confronted him, Aaron? Why haven't you talked to your father about how you feel?"

Talk to him. Ha! He talked to his father, all right: if he picked up the phone when Aaron called to talk to his half-brother, Luke. Once every few months he and his father would have stunted conversations about the unbearable traffic or about Luke's scholastic achievements. They talked on birthdays and holidays, too, to say, Happy Birthday, Dad/Aaron, and to exchange paltry gifts bought without forethought and plain brown cards with predictable drawings of cakes and candles that said nothing beyond the plain wishes they had already exchanged. But they didn't *talk*. Ever. Their bond to each other was a formality that engaged them only because of the documented fact of their genetic link, indisputable in Aaron's hospital records and on his birth certificate, but Aaron didn't like being his father's son any more than he supposed his father liked being his father.

For one thing, they didn't even know each other. Yeah, Aaron had spent some time living with him and his new wife for a few months when he was thirteen, but it turned out to be a bad idea. He couldn't accept his father's strictness, his inflexible rules, his dictatorial presence, and then Aaron had forgotten his stepmother's birthday, and that was the end of it all.

Father was shouting at him, pointing a finger at his face, bitter prophecies about Aaron's presumed *direction in life* flying out of his mouth with spittle and rage.

"It's just another day," Aaron had said. "She's not even my mother."

"You're an irresponsible punk."

"Like father, like son," Aaron had said. It's not as though he hadn't seen the veined hollows at his father's temples or the flush and sweat disrupting the smoothness of the older man's flat cheeks, but all he knew at that moment was a sudden and inexplicable hilarity. He could feel his own lips trembling with it even before he'd finished the last words. And then he had laughed, laughed hard, guffaws pushing out of his lungs and into his father's face. That's when his father had picked him up by the shirt collar and by the belt of his pants and thrown him down the staircase. Aaron had hit the balustrade and fallen on his left knee, which still hurt him to this day, especially while playing basketball. Then he'd gotten up, straightened his shirt as though he were fine, and clenched his teeth back against the pain and the tears. He walked into his room and packed his clothes in a bag, not even looking at what he'd thrown in there: foolish stuff, like a book he'd never read, and his half-brother's Nerf ball, and shirts, a lot of them dirty, and not even a single useful sweater. He hadn't been thinking, really, about what he might need, about what he was actually packing. He'd only been thinking about hurting his father. The outdoor gauge had marked six degrees below zero that day, and the wind pushed the temperature maybe another fifteen degrees below that. Aaron had walked in his boots and parka through the living room and out the front door, making as much noise as he could, knocking things around, cursing the weather, slamming the door as he walked out. He'd walked all the way to the bus station, foundering into the deep snow, ice seeping into his boots, wetting his socks, and the wind freezing the tears on his face and nose. He kept expecting his father's Toyota Celica to pull up honking, a window rolling down, a door coming ajar. He'd nursed that fantasy all the way to New York City, and then when he'd gotten off the bus at Times Square with only three dollars to eat on and five quarter to call his mother in Florida, he stopped thinking about it and never thought about it again.

"And anyway, I'm not a young man, you know?" Aaron's father said over the phone. "I'd slow you down."

"It doesn't matter," Aaron said. "I could prepare you for the trip if you wanted to go."

"I don't have the gear."

"I could give you most of what you need. I still have Garret's backpack and an extra sleeping bag."

"Ah, so Garret is coming?"

Aaron took the sudden enthusiasm in his father's voice like a punch in the face.

"No," he said, exhaling, "Garret is not coming," and the breath that came out of him hurt his lungs somehow.

A picture of Garret was in his head. Garret. His older brother. Garret in his head as he looked ten years ago: dirty hair, hilarious smile, ruddy cheeks dusted with sand the way he looked in a picture Aaron took of him in the Utah desert.

"We could ask Luke to come with us, though."

There was breathing on the line, and then, "No. You know how I feel about that. It's too dangerous."

"How do you know if you've never tried?"

There was no reply from the other end.

Aaron massaged his temples and closed his eyes. There was Garret again, standing blond and tousled in dusty hiking boots, his parka slung over his shoulder, a hand holding back a sheaf of dirty hair from his high forehead. He'd look different, today, of course: heavier, dirtier, bluer around the eyes, and lips stone cold with boredom.

There had been a time when he and Garret had been close, but it didn't last long. When they were kids, Garret was Father's favorite. He could do no wrong in Father's eyes. Even long after the divorce, before Aaron's memories began, Father had had a soft spot for Garret – the only reason, perhaps, he'd remained with Mom as long as he had. Garret knew it. Mom knew it. Aaron knew it—too well. But Garret had grown up failing everyone's expectations. He'd dropped out of school and married too soon and later, regretting it, estranged his wife and child, and divorced, and remarried, and had another child, and dropped out of school again, and become a used car salesman and a drunkard, proving to be as much a failure as a husband and father as he was as a brother, and for this, as for many other things, Aaron blamed his father.

Still, he hated the way things went around in circles, just like social workers and psychologists said. It took the humanity out of suffering and turned it into a cipher, a statistic, a blurb in someone's scholastic research.

"Another reason to talk to your father," Dr. Piper told him.

"He'd never give me the time of day," Aaron had retorted.

"Take him someplace quiet where there won't be any interruptions. Go on a trip with him. Go fishing. Do something both of you like to do."

". . . and I don't know if I'm suited for this kind of thing," his father was saying.

"Why don't you just say it straight out, Dad," Aaron cut in, his snapping voice quickly truncating his father's stream of excuses. "Just say you don't want to go."

There was a pause, and then, "Look . . ." and more breathing, and then, "I want to go."

"Really?" It didn't come out sounding like a question. "You want to go, but . . . ?"

"But I don't know if I can."

Aaron had to shut his eyes as if against a breath of dust. He bit into his lips and held his fist clenched and realized that more than anything he wanted to hit his father, hurt him somehow, hurt him and overcome him and then hurt him some more.

"Well . . ." his father said. "Well, maybe . . . I'll see what I can do."

"When? When am I going to find out? Tomorrow? Next month? Next year?"

"Hold on," said his father. And Aaron was put on hold. Long enough for him to think of things he'd not thought about in a long time. Those six months at his father's house . . . the de rigueur trip to church every Sunday . . . *No, I don't want to . . . That's just not an option* . . . and then standing in a corner, with his face to the wall, and books under his arms, and his legs still smarting from the welts his father's belt had left on his calves . . . *You stay right there and think about it for a while. And don't you even think about dropping those books* . . . and his arms ached hour after hour, and his pride throbbed, and his hands wanted to give up, and his father's stare felt like a laser burning a hole into the back of his head . . .

"I think we can arrange something." His father's voice came to him distorted, like a memory instead of the stark, halogen-lit present it occupied.

"What? Are you sure?"

"Yes. I think I can work something out here at the office."

"New Mexico, then?"

"New Mexico," said his father.

And it was done, a done deal. Aaron rubbed his eyes. He'd expected relief, or excitement, or worry to wash over him as soon as he hung up, but instead there was that same nasty cocktail of anger and tension that flavored their every encounter.

2

Tom slipped his arms into the backpack that Aaron had lent him and was surprised by the weight of the burden on his knees and back. He had practiced on a treadmill every day for a few weeks, had even agreed to meet Aaron in the park near his house, and had walked around an hour or two with weights in his backpack to get used to the burden, but today the pack felt different.

He didn't want Aaron to see him falter, and instead of leaning forward as his body wanted him to, he buckled his knees and then bounced straight up, his thumbs firmly slipped under the shoulder straps and a satisfied grin on his face. Aaron stared back at him, a tuft of reddish hair flopping over his eyebrow, his lower lip disappearing momentarily under his teeth.

"You OK, Dad?"

Tom didn't know if the concern in his son's voice was genuine, but momentarily he wondered if Aaron had made the pack heavier on purpose, and it suddenly became important that he not give him the satisfaction of knowing how heavy it felt.

"Just fine," he said and slowly became conscious that he was wiping his forehead with the back of his hand, the heat already drawing beads of sweat from his skin. He hid the betraying hand in his pocket and waited for Aaron to lead. Aaron glanced at the sign that announced the entrance to Bandelier National Monument, then glanced back at Tom and grinned, clapping his hands together.

"I'm excited about this," he announced with that same note of falsity that had rankled Tom in Aaron's mother. Without another word, Aaron headed along a dusty path, Tom stumbling behind with an awkward and strained waddle, all his training and preparation proving instantly inadequate. They weren't even at the trailhead yet, and here already he had to stop, easing his pack down to readjust his waist strap. On the airplane, Aaron had mentioned something about submitting their hiking plan to the Visitor's Center and registering for what he called a backcountry permit, and Tom assumed the quaint building where his son was headed was where those permits would be obtained. When he caught up to the building and went inside, Aaron was already talking to the ranger on duty.

"There he is," Aaron said with a nod in Tom's direction. He and the ranger smiled back at him, the hint of a personal joke in their identical grins.

"How's it going, Dad?" Aaron called out to him. Tom wordlessly unlatched the waist strap and eased his pack to the wood-boarded floor, and after a moment of their silent staring at him, he said he had to use the bathroom. When he came out, Aaron was still chuckling with the ranger, their heads bent over a map. Tom caught random words. *Cliff dwellings. Loop through Alamo Canyon marked very difficult . . . 2,000-foot elevation gain . . . Waterproof treatment for the creek.* Aaron looked genuinely excited, a smile on his handsome face to match his breathless questions. The ranger was talking fast and low, sharing a comfortable jargon that spoke to his knowledge of the site as well as his confidence in Aaron's experience. Though he understood their words, Tom failed to understand the general meaning. He suddenly realized that he was entirely at his son's mercy, Aaron's skill and knowledge of wildlife his only assurance of safety. He knew this was part of the reason for Aaron's invitation: to prove him inadequate in some way and perhaps to boast of Aaron's own skill and self-sufficiency. He hadn't let that bother him and didn't want to start now. He trusted the Lord would look after him in this endeavor. Still, looking at his son next to the ranger, Tom experienced an uncertain feeling. Perhaps it was the way Aaron smiled or his body posture, he didn't know. He looked like—Tom held his chin, drumming his fingers on his lips—not like any of his sons . . . more like his mother than Garret, yet more like himself than even his youngest, Luke, whose face features were exactly like his own.

Luke had Aaron in his head, and he was the reason Tom had finally agreed to go on this trip. Luke was possessed by his half-brother the way a teenager is possessed by the image of a superhero. He could idolize Aaron because the brothers seldom saw each other, spoke only on the phone every few weeks through long sessions that were mostly about Aaron's latest girlfriends or vacation. Tom was disgusted by those conversations, had overheard something once about a girl who wanted Aaron to go see her at a college, and Aaron had said, ". . . because she refused to suck my cock, so I told her she wasn't worth it." Tom had picked up the phone by mistake in the first place, but after that small tidbit he had no desire to listen to anything more. He heard it all from Luke later, anyway. Aaron did this, and Aaron did that. And did it stop at the talk? When Aaron took up guitar, Luke used his summer job savings to sign up for drum lessons. When Aaron took a job as a systems analyst, Luke changed his intended major to information systems on his college application. When Aaron took up rafting, Luke wanted a kayak for his birthday. When Aaron began hiking and mountain climbing, Luke wanted to go with him.

Tom said no.

Luke at seventeen was a gawky child, clumsy with his body, as though it were a suit two sizes too big. He bumped into the edges of furniture, stumbled off door steps, walked into screen doors. He could quote episodes and characters by date and issue number from the vintage Superman comic books he collected the way most kids his age would quote football stats. He was too tall and serious to be picked on by the other kids at school, but he was a stick on sneakers. Whenever Tom looked at Luke, he wanted to wrap his soul around the kid like a force field, the bony frame of his son's body a fragile thing in his eyes, dangerously exposed to the perilous impermanence of the world.

He felt no such apprehension for Aaron, whose arrogance always succeeded in blasting any sympathy Tom tried to muster for him.

Tom had tried to reason with him. He'd called Aaron on the phone the day before his trip to Mount McKinley in Alaska, where Aaron was going climbing with a friend from college. Luke had desperately wanted to go along, lobbying for permission day and night. When Tom made his decision final, Luke for the first time in his life became disrespectful. He talked back at Tom, even shouted. "You're afraid of everything! You just want to keep me locked up in here until I rot!" He'd slammed the door and kicked things around, then refused to come out of his room for dinner.

Tom wouldn't ask Aaron not to go, knowing that Aaron took particular pleasure in recklessness and in causing consternation, but of course he'd wished he could have stopped him, too. He had read the books and seen the Imax film of that expedition to Everest. He wasn't a fool and knew the dangers of those places and those types of sports.

"I want you to be careful when you're out there," he'd told Aaron nonetheless, hoping that those peace-seeking words might set the mood for the ensuing conversation.

There had been a protracted pause at the other end that Tom had mistakenly understood as Aaron feeling touched. But then Tom mentioned Luke.

"He's so impressionable. He wants to do everything you do. I don't want him out there. It's too dangerous."

And then Aaron turned into what Tom ought to have expected: not a mature grown man with sense and responsibility but a vengeful predator weaned on rage and on his mother's bitterness, a young punk who understood nothing except his own rapacious needs.

"You can't tell him what to do!" he'd shouted. "He's a man. He can make his own decisions."

"He's seventeen and my son."

"In a few months he'll be eighteen. You can't stop him."

What Aaron had really meant, of course, was something else. It wasn't Luke he couldn't stop, it was Aaron. Luke was only the sorry casualty of Aaron's rage.

When Aaron was thirteen and living with them, he seemed to hate even just the down on Tom's knuckles. He'd sit across from him at the dinner table, staring for minutes on end at Tom's hands or over his eyes, as if at a dark spot right above Tom's nose, playing a sort of psychological ping pong with the shrugs and snide little smiles he answered to every question Tom posed to him. Aaron's pulpy mouth was set at the corners in a permanent frown, his eyebrows furrowed over his huge, conspiring eyes. But he hated his stepmother most of all. If Rowan said, "Don't wear that dirty shirt," Aaron would pour lighter fluid on it and burn it in the backyard. If Rowan said, "Cut your hair," Aaron would shave himself bald. Rowan was afraid of him, but most of all, she was afraid of his influence on Luke. Tom, on the other hand, was most afraid of Aaron's stubbornness. One night he'd belted Aaron's legs for so long his arms ached. He'd wanted to get a cry out of Aaron, a plea for surrender, but Aaron couldn't be broken. He'd wince and even occasionally let out a moan or two, but he wouldn't cry, and he wouldn't beg, and finally Tom had to stop, defeated by the red welts on Aaron's legs. He remembered a secret desire to bend down and kiss those welts, which disturbed him even more than the way Aaron had shivered, sucking in his moans.

Had he behaved like Aaron with his own father, Tom would have been beaten to a pulp. When he was eleven, he had accidentally set fire to the living room carpet. His father had beaten him until he lost consciousness. But Tom didn't have the heart to hurt Aaron that way. Already the belting was a weight he'd taken to the church pews week after week, his knees bruised with the long time kneeling, his lips dry with the constant prayer. Merciful God! At least there was something to be said about Aaron; he was a warrior. Tom's own spirit had been as strong as steel in youth, but where had it led him? To a bad marriage and two children he wasn't ready to father or to support, to the estrangement from his church and the shame of his family. He'd only wanted to spare Aaron that. He'd explained this to God over and over, but Aaron's will was stronger than Tom's intentions.

Aaron had stopped talking to the ranger and turned toward him, a shuffle to his left foot giving him a kind of swagger that Tom recognized as Aaron's particular walk. Aaron's head was still bent over the map he and the ranger had been studying together.

"Sam and I figured the best way to go would be through this twenty-eight-mile loop," he said. He'd used the ranger's first name with such familiarity that Tom would have thought they were accomplices in murder. "That will take us around to all the major sites. We estimated we could make it in about two and a half days." Aaron stood close to him, spreading the map open for him to see. The map had thick red felt-pen marks that circled names like Frijoles Canyon, Yapashi Ruin, Tyuonyi Overlook. "What do you think?" he asked, as though he intended Tom to have a say in this. "Says here it's a strenuous walk in some parts."

"I'm up for it," Tom said. "God willing."

Aaron folded his map and placed it into one of the outer pockets of his pack, then eased into the arm straps, his hands fastening the waist strap tight. As he walked out he threw a "Thanks, Sam" over his shoulder and a "Take care, buddy," like Sam the ranger was his fraternity brother.

The ranger lifted his hand and nodded. "You folks take care now," he said.

Outside the Visitor's Center, Aaron called out a "You OK, Dad?" before disappearing behind a scanty shrub that marked the trailhead at the edge of the parking lot. Tom nodded, the heat a substance pressing around the surface of his body, as if conspiring with the open sky, the mountains, and the canyons to diminish him. He had drunk so much water in the truck at Aaron's insistence that he could feel his stomach swishing with every step. He wanted to look up and take in the grandness of the volcanic projections that bent their gnarly beige bodies as if to bow in reverence to the great sky, but he found his gaze returning to the small stones, the sticks and dust and rolling debris at his feet. Before long he was winding through shady groves of thick pine trees, dry shrubs and creepers scratching his elbows and calves as he passed through them. Aaron was only about fifteen feet ahead, his pace more confident than Tom's, though occasionally he'd slow down and complain that the trails weren't well kept. When a clearing opened up before them, Aaron came to a standstill. Tom lifted his head, his breathing already loud as it scratched out of his dry throat. In the distance, from under a thick ring of smoke, he could discern darkened patches on the side of a mountain, the scorching of the summer fires that still raged at the edges of Bandelier Monument and into the Sangre de Cristo mountain range. Aaron had wanted to head to the Carson National Forest first, had talked excitedly about climbing Wheeler Peak, the highest elevation in New Mexico, and bathing in the thermal springs in the forest, but after the long ride from the hotel, they had climbed out of the rented truck only to be turned back by the forest police at the entrance of the park, the fires having raged out of control.

Aaron had stomped his foot and spat on the ground, hands on hips as he shook his head at the thick, smoky haze, his eyes lost in some angry reverie. Tom had secretly felt relieved at the same time as he was disappointed. He didn't know if he could manage the climb up Wheeler Peak, in his fifties and without much experience with the sport. Still, he'd wanted to prove to both Luke and

Aaron that he could be open-minded, that he wasn't just an old man talking out of his ears. Besides, he figured if he could satisfy this whim of Aaron's, perhaps Aaron would spare Luke his petty vengeance.

"We can come back another time," he'd told Aaron, trying to clap him on the shoulder.

Aaron had scampered away, managing to miss his touch.

"Yeah, right!" he'd bitterly spat as he climbed inside the truck. He'd slammed the door hard and worked the starter before Tom even had a chance to climb into the passenger seat.

"It's nothing to get so worked-up about," Tom had said as he settled in the truck.

"I'd be surprised if anything did upset you, Dad," Aaron had said, slapping one hand on the stick shift and the other on the steering wheel, a grimace that disrupted the grace of his high cheekbones as he reversed out of the parking lot. He'd said something else under his breath, but Tom didn't understand and wasn't going to ask about it either. Aaron gunned through the winding state road toward the highway, his eyebrows set low, his forehead wrinkled.

"What's this all about?" Tom finally said through his teeth, holding on to his seat as Aaron made the truck swerve with a too-tight turn onto the highway. He itched to push Aaron aside and wrap his fingers around the steering wheel, even if it meant crashing into a ditch off the side of the road. He'd gladly have it out with Aaron right there, man to man, the old-fashioned way. He wasn't about to let his son hold him hostage.

"What's it all about?" Aaron said, a hypocrite's smile exposing his teeth. "It's about you, Dad. It's always about you."

Tom felt a knot of tension forming in his chest, then move down to his stomach and legs.

"Stop the truck, Aaron," he said.

"What's that?" Aaron shouted over the strained engine, but to Tom he sounded like a man who knew he'd gone too far. It appeased Tom somehow, but not enough.

"You stop the truck," he repeated, the calm in his voice a more sophisticated kind of rage. Aaron hesitated, then eased his foot off the accelerator.

"You want to get out? Here?"

"Yes."

Tom looked straight ahead, watched the asphalt disappear under the hood, miles of road swallowed beneath them, excreted at high speed under the truck bed in the side-view mirror. Aaron slowed down and coasted into the emergency lane as if about to stop, then sped up again. They said nothing more to each other for as long as they stayed on the road. Then in Taos, Tom got out of the truck, fumbling for his jacket, his wallet, and the paperback Bible he had stored in the glove compartment. Wordlessly, he walked into the first restaurant he saw. He flirted with the waitress, settled in a booth by the window, and ordered himself a sizeable meal. After a short while, Aaron walked in after him but didn't follow him to the booth. He stared at Tom, shifting his weight on his legs until the waitress asked him if he wanted a table, then shook his head and walked out. Tom asked the waitress for the newspaper at the concession stand, tipping her a few dollars for the errand. After he'd read the newspaper front to end, he ordered coffee and peach pie and read Psalms in the Bible. Several hours later, Aaron slid into the booth across from him, elbows on table, a tour guide instantly spreading open in his hands.

"I got it all figured out," he said, an easy smile spreading on his face as though Tom were a girl that Aaron wanted to bring to bed. "Bandelier National Monument. Look here. 6,066-foot elevation gain. Pretty cool, huh? *Rife* with archaeological ruins. You like that, don't you? Anasazi dwellings, hieroglyphs. There's plenty to see. Then if there's time, we could drive to . . ." He breathed in, and his chest filled up as if he were trying to show himself stronger, somehow. ". . . White Sands National Park." He pointed at a picture of pristine white sand dunes, speckled with round tufts of shrubs like the pubes of an adolescent. He slid the guidebook across the table to Tom, and with the other hand he gently tugged at the Bible in Tom's hands.

Gazing out from the clearing, Tom's thoughts began to feel absorbed by the landscape, his sight clinging to the steep facade of the canyon and to the blackened face of the mountain far away. The sun beat on his forehead. Still Tom thought he could make himself not notice, if he only just concentrated again on the wind-pecked ravines cupping the course of the Frijoles Creek below. Aaron's face seemed tense with concentration.

"Do you hear that?"

Tom held his raspy breath. At first he could only hear the breathing of the wind, gusts that played the cavities of the curved and beaten rocks like whispering flutes, but after a moment a faint, persistent drumming punctured through the smoother melodies of the backcountry.

"Woodpecker," Aaron said. He turned to face Tom, and his eyes seemed wider somehow above a flickering and uncertain smile. "Already at work on the surviving tree trunks. Fires are important to them. They rely on the bugs that live inside recently burnt trees." Then, as if he had said nothing, heard nothing, Aaron resumed the trail. Tom felt a pinching pain above his pelvis, right where the top edge of the waist strap dug into his soft muscle. The pack seemed to be bumping into the back of his head with every shaky step, his ankles wobbling over the rubble at his feet. They hadn't been on the trail very long, and yet he felt exhausted. Sweat was streaming from his hair into his eyes and over his lips. His shirt was wet and heavy, clinging to his chest, though he was wearing polypropylene like Aaron had told him and not the more comfortable cotton he would have liked to have. The hair on his arms and legs seemed to be burning right off him. He felt the sting of the sun as though someone poked him at intervals with a lighted match.

After some time, they stopped briefly at the Anasazi cave dwellings. Aaron pointed out the cavities in the multicolored rock formations that were pliant enough to be dug into by the native population hundreds of years ago. Tom had a difficult time distinguishing the dwellings from the natural cavities, but he nodded and quietly marveled at the ingenuity of primitive men. Aaron was excited. He took out his camera and took pictures. A rabbit poked his head out of a hole and hopped a few paces, as if curious about Aaron's presence on his turf, then zigzagged across the ruin, his white tail like a strange desert flower flashing through the dusty rubble. Aaron chased him a considerable distance, his feet shuffling over the rocks. Once Tom watched him lose his balance, his arms swinging and flailing as if to reach for invisible railings. Tom winced, holding his breath. But Aaron regained his footing and returned to Tom with a satisfied grin on his face, brandishing the disposable camera.

They had some water and a granola bar; then quickly resumed the pace, Aaron bustling over his GPS device with the seriousness of an astronomer. They took a path down a canyon that eventually, Aaron claimed, would take them to more interesting ruins. Tom felt the fatigue begin to clamp at his limbs like the hand of God, trying to hold him back, but he said nothing.

They traveled over the mesa top, saying little to each other, perhaps as much to save their breath and moisture as for lack of things to share. With their ascent into the first canyon, bushes and agaves began to replace the thick clumps of pine trees, and he felt more exposed than ever. Aaron was already a thumb-size blur of color up ahead, now and then disappearing behind a cactus, the latches and zippers on his backpack shimmering intermittently along the path. Tom tried to hasten his pace but fell back to a slow stroll. His feet tested the ground gingerly as it became drier, dustier, and steeper. His toes scraped the inside of his boot, already giving him a hint of pain. He thought about the poles strapped on the back of his pack and wanted to ask Aaron to stop so he could relieve himself of their weight and use them to maintain his balance as he moved along the trail. Aaron was not in sight for several moments during which Tom had time to think of his blood pressure, of twenty-two million strokes occurring every year in the United States, and of the effects of excess heat and exhaustion on a man his age. Then Aaron was there again, waiting for him by several tall, peaked columns.

"Strange, huh?" Aaron said as soon as Tom was within hearing range.

"Hold on," Tom called back, afraid Aaron might resume the trail before Tom had a chance to rest. When he reached Aaron he was panting. A curious shame prevented him from asking Aaron for a rest. Instead he managed, "What are they?" gasping for air and willing his heartbeat to slow.

"Just tuff," Aaron said. "Some kind of volcanic substance. Natural formations." Aaron cupped a hand over his forehead and grimaced at Tom through the glare. "I think you need some water," he declared, then fumbled with the pack on Tom's back for his water bottle. "Dad . . ." He stopped and sucked in his breath as if he'd seen a snake inside his pack and was trying to prevent panic. "Dad, is your pack comfortable?" He came around to face him and looked at him with a tentative respect. He looked much like Garret suddenly, shy and judicious, hoping to be forgiven his trespasses. Tom remembered that face vividly and the many school meetings he'd had to endure, as well as the smugness of inept school counselors who would explain his first son's outstanding test scores and his exhaustive detention record with ready-made phrases like "repressed rage" and "fear of abandonment" and other handy labels that seemed aimed more at his failure as a parent than at a solution for his son.

"It seems a little heavy," Tom confessed, jiggling his shoulders as if the problem were nothing more than a wrinkle on his jacket.

"I don't think it's properly adjusted. It looks like it's digging into your waist. Sit down over there."

Why had he thought of Garret just now? Tom felt that old pain like rheumatism in bad weather. Ah, Garret, his first and most painful failure. Tom had done what he could. He'd attended counseling, subjecting himself to the insidious questions of strangers who hid their malice behind their degrees. ("I'm still unclear, Mr. Wayne. How does belting a child's legs really relate to his maturity?") He had offered his support long-distance with his hard-earned money and, when the court allowed, with temporary custody, trying to make a Christian out of his son, reading the Gospel to him at the dinner table, taking the time to foster his child's spiritual education the way his father had done with him when he'd been young. He had even paid Garret's expensive tuition at a private technical school where his son studied engineering for six years, failing course after course while exhausting Tom's savings, ambitions, and hopes—and for what? The complacent, pimply, pregnant teenage girl who became Garret's first wife, the used car dealership where Garret burned his degree, and a grandson he never got to see because of lawsuits and family feuds. After Garret he just didn't want to try. For a long time he wanted only to push the past aside and forget the mistake of his first wife and the two children she had blackmailed him with, first into marriage, with Garret, and later into staying, with Aaron. Sometimes he thought, If only he could go back in time and walk away from that first mistake . . .

Tom was glad enough for the lull and even gladder when Aaron handed him the water bottle. He hadn't realized how thirsty he was until the warm trickle hit his tongue. Then his lips greedily sought the nipple, and he sucked with little control, feeling the paste of dried spit wash away from his palate. Aaron fumbled with the straps, fussing around him, his face red and sweaty and swelling with heat.

"I'd like to use my poles," Tom suggested. Aaron bustled along as though he hadn't heard, but a few moments later Tom had the poles in his hands, and Aaron sucked from his own water bottle, which he'd adjusted on a pouch to be within reach without having to remove his pack.

"You must've been very uncomfortable," Aaron declared. "You should've told me."

Tom turned his face toward the sun and looked at it hard, relieved by the sting it caused his eyeballs. He felt the skin around his jaw and between his eyebrows bunched so tight it almost hurt.

"Those who are in the flesh cannot please God. But you are not in the flesh; you are in the spirit, if only the Spirit of God dwells in you." He turned back to look at Aaron, his mood improved by the recitation. "Romans. The words of St. Paul."

Aaron remained still, his face a muscular contraction difficult to read. He nodded and looked ahead to the trail, where the mesa tops above them shed thin veils of dust with the blowing wind, and where a haze from the distant fires still hovered in spite of a beautiful day. Or maybe he was looking elsewhere; Tom couldn't tell, but it made no difference anyway. The words of the Lord had come to Tom as from a hidden spring inside, refreshing him with their beauty and poetry, and now the fatigue washed over him like a balm, teasing him with a gentle peace and a connection to Aaron he hadn't felt before.

"In the flesh without God, in the spirit with God," Aaron repeated suddenly, a tension in the tone of his voice that broke the spell of their communion. "So was it in the spirit that you married Mom, or was it just in the flesh?"

Tom felt the heat clapping on him full force, the beads of sweat returning to his face.

"In those days I wasn't very religious," he tersely admitted, standing up from the rock he'd been sitting on, slapping off ants that had crawled up the hair on his legs.

"Dad, wait," Aaron said, a gawkiness to his posture that suddenly made him look more like Luke. "I guess I just . . . I tried to understand . . ."

Tom poked the poles into the ground to test them. They had a nice spring to them that would help ease the impact on his knees.

"The pack feels much better this way," he said briskly, leading as he resumed the trail.

The feeling of closeness had evaporated with the heat, and his privacy felt intruded upon as though it were a lawyer asking him these questions and not his son. A part of him recognized this as sad and regrettable, but then again, why should he feel guilty? Because talk-show jargon had made criminals out of old-fashioned parents who valued discipline, respect, and authority above those dramatic, humiliating confessions? Communication. Openness. Understanding. Television antics that were not so much effective as they were fashionable. He would've never dared ask such personal questions of his father.

In his irritation he had hastened his pace, and before he was aware of it he had traveled a sizeable distance ahead of Aaron. There on the path, sidling toward him from under a huge, sun-bleached log, slithered a movie-perfect rattlesnake, its tail glistening in the sunlight, rattling to transmit its reptilian displeasure. Tom quickly crouched to the ground, groped with his hand for the largest rock he could find, and threw it at the snake. The rock stomped on the ground, missing the snake by several inches and raising a spit of dust. The snake lifted its triangular head and hissed at Tom, its spiked tongue flickering and disappearing into its beaded snake head. Then it slithered off under the log and off the trail. Aaron was just a pace behind Tom now, his breath quick and agitated.

"Don't do that," he panted. "Don't." He held a hand to his forehead as though something extraordinarily foolish had just happened. "Dad, we're the strangers here. Not the other way around. This is *his* environment."

Tom was struck with the absurdity of this reproach. He thought Aaron would be grateful that Tom had scared the snake away, and he felt genuinely hurt.

"We try to leave the trail unspoiled," Aaron said. "Any change to the environment may have an impact beyond our understanding. Even just that rock," he said, pointing accusingly at the stone. "We don't touch anything until we get to the campsite. OK?"

Aaron must have understood the resentment on Tom's face, because he didn't wait for acknowledgment and instead resumed the lead down the path. Before long he had taken what Aaron earlier had called a switchback and was soon out of sight. The trail zigzagged gently down the canyon, taking some steep turns where it was easy to lose sight of someone even only twenty feet ahead. The descent seemed steeper, but the poles were helping Tom balance his weight. With the pack well adjusted he felt a little of his energies and enthusiasm return, a desire to show his arrogant son that even at his age he still retained his masculine resilience acting as an efficient fuel for the endeavor.

As a young man he'd been sought out by girls for his looks and his manliness. Captain of the wrestling team. All-country track champion. ROTC scholarship. He had reveled in the touches of girls who wanted to trace his pectorals with their frail fingers, kiss the tendons of his taurine neck with their petal lips. He recognized in retrospect the vanity of it, the false idolatry inherent in the love of his own image, but in his youth he'd drawn a unique and addictive pleasure from it. Lisette had loved his maleness as much as all the others, her adoration shimmering under her thick red eyelashes, but Lisette was different, with her strawberry blond hair, her gentle Canadian accent, the phrases of French she'd break into when, in her frustration, she would try to find the right English words. She'd called him *mon cher*, kissed him on the cheeks. When they'd first started dating, he'd been hesitant to get out of his car to ring the doorbell, intimidated by the parlor grand in the picture window of her parents' Victorian house, its lid raised and glittery like the wet inverted rudder of an enormous ship. Lisette played Mozart on the piano, studied ballet with Ballanchine. She wasn't like the loose-haired blonds in tie-dyes Tom had fondled in bars and at open-air concerts, hating them for their liberal and passé politics and loving them for their braless breasts and diaphanous shirts. Lisette made him think of things he had not dared aspire to: Persian rugs and parlor pianos, collected paintings and custom architecture. He was going to study engineering, and she was going to study medicine. They would be rich and buy a house and have only one child who would speak two languages and be raised by a live-in nanny. Lisette would help Tom avoid the fallout of *southernness* that contaminated the speech and manners of an ambitious boy from northern Florida. She would help him become a man of the world. But then Lisette got pregnant before she'd even started college, and he'd had to drop out of school to marry her and support her and Garret. Their families had disowned them because she was Catholic and he was Lutheran, and they had married in court. At that time his faith meant little to him, but he immediately missed the ways and traditions of his family and regretted having given them up so easily. In a matter of months he saw his dream fade with the cloth diapers Lisette washed in the bathtub to save money and the dollars she hid in empty coffee cans like a country girl. He came to hate her odd Canadian accent and the hasty French she spoke on the phone with her friends so he wouldn't understand what she said, and what he'd once thought of as sophistication he later came to recognize as a vulgar kind of affectation, even more deplorable than his own southernness because it was as much pretentious as it was false. He had already made up his mind to leave her when she told him she was pregnant with Aaron. There was a mischievous sort of satisfaction in her eyes, and he couldn't help but think that she had somehow managed it on purpose. As if being an assistant electrician and living in a one-bedroom apartment in the slums weren't bad enough.

The trail had now turned to open country, and he could see several cacti and desert plants. He recognized one from Aaron's tour guide called a tree cholla that had purple, waxlike, thick-petaled flowers blooming from angled, scaly prongs. If there was wildlife, he couldn't discern it, except for the occasional rotting carcass of a rabbit, or a skunk, or something unrecognizable and the flies and buzzards that feasted on it. He couldn't even see his own son, though the path ahead was clear for several miles. From time to time he'd hear Aaron's voice travel back to him on the heated wind with an "Are you all right, Dad?" He'd answer back a grumbling "I'll make it," but secretly, in spite of the strain, in spite of the breath now burning his lungs, he was enjoying himself. He didn't know how far he had traveled, but it must have been several miles, and the sun felt hotter, the heat heavier, so that he knew it to be late morning or early afternoon. He refused to look at his watch so as not to spoil the spell of grandness, of the harsh beauty before him. The canyon walls had turned a deep kind of brown, basalt, he remembered reading in the trail guide. The wind caused a curious sensation on his burning skin as though someone, a ghost, a spirit, breathed at intervals on his neck or brushed the back of his hand. The sensation was as convincing as the glare of the sun from the rocks in his eyes, and he felt confused, not knowing if he should be frightened, or awed, or mystified.

Eventually, he came to a creek, where Aaron was waiting for him, his pack at his side. The vegetation had once again changed, as had the terrain. It was moister and softer, with lush grass and high reeds, and the smell of damp, of moss and young grass, was gratifying. Ahead, Tom could see more woodland, where it would be shadier than here, but Aaron was comfortably lolling on the bank of the creek, a foot dangling in the water. He was dipping a white cylindrical device, which he had connected with a see-through plastic tube to an almost empty bottle, into the dull, shallow water of the creek.

"This water is full of clay," he said, not bothering with a greeting, "and our water supplies aren't exceptional."

"Is that bad?" Tom asked.

"It is if the filter clogs." Aaron's elbows suddenly jerked as he sucked in spit from his closed lips, then he lifted the filter over his eyes and squinted, his mouth hardening into an odd grimace. "I saw an Abert squirrel," he said, as if to finalize the news.

Abert squirrel. Tom tried to remember if he should know what that was.

"I only recognized it because of those weird ears, all pointy and dark." A tenuous smile blossomed on Aaron's hot face, and Tom, quite unexpectedly, welled up with gratitude. The feeling so embarrassed him that it became a weight, a sort of clump in his stomach. He was afraid Aaron might see it, so he turned away, clumsily slipping loose the straps around his waist and shoulders.

"Don't get too comfortable," Aaron warned. "We have a lot of mileage yet."

"Did you get a picture?"

Aaron didn't answer. He'd been that way as a teenager, too:

ignoring questions, diminishing people with his indifference, his perpetual pout. But maybe, Tom conjectured, maybe Aaron had simply forgotten the squirrel already and didn't know what Tom had meant, or maybe he simply hadn't heard, tuned in so deeply to his task. Aaron must have liked animals very much, how he'd acted with the snake, and now giving news of the squirrel with as much seriousness as he gave news of the filter. Tom had a vague recollection of Aaron talking excitedly about neighbors' dogs, naming the species and listing their characteristics. *And the Joneses on Pine Street have a Doberman, which is Hitler's breed, you know? And his brain grows bigger than his skull, so that when those dogs get big they get vicious, and then they go mad* . . . There had also been a white cat Aaron had brought home from a school fair and then given to Luke as a gift. What happened to the cat? He couldn't remember. He'd just found a hole in his memory, and Aaron was the filling, and he couldn't decide if it was a good thing. How Aaron had chased that rabbit back at the ruins . . . *It's only a rabbit*, he wanted to shout when Aaron's feet had started slipping from the slope, his backpack dangerously weighing him down, his otherwise limber movements turned awkward by the heavy load and even embarrassing to look at. A rabbit. He could have slipped and fallen and broken a leg or sprained an ankle, and then what? Tom felt resentful, suddenly, for the rabbit chase, but then he also felt giddy and wanted very much to laugh.

Instead he took off his boot and then his outer cotton sock and then his wicking nylon sock and looked at his toes wiggling in the sun. They were red. And soon they would be blistery.

Aaron crouched over Tom's foot and picked at a toe with two fingers, careful like a clock repairman. "You're going to blister if you don't take care of that. Are your boots tight enough?"

Tom looked down at his other boot, helpless and childish. Aaron tugged at the laces and shook his head. "No. They're not. I'd bet your other foot is blistering as well."

The gratitude peeled away into a vulgar shame. Tom mumbled, removing his straw hat to wipe his forehead. "It doesn't hurt yet."

Aaron put away the filter and then fumbled with his backpack and finally treated Tom's blisters with moleskin, then put a piece of duct tape over it to prevent it from falling off, he said. He insisted they needed to get going, that they had already lost a lot of time, but still he untied the damp bandanna from his neck and wet it in the creek and tied it around Tom's forehead with such delicate gestures that Tom's scalp tingled. When Tom was a kid his mother would draw letters on his back with her finger, and he'd always guess the letters wrong on purpose so that she would keep touching him, her fingers poking gently between the muscles of his back. His eyes felt moist, and he looked at Aaron to see if he'd been discovered, but Aaron's gaze was far away, as always, concentrated, intelligent hazel eyes just low-cast enough to conceal whatever it was he felt. There was a thin layer of sweat glistening on Aaron's upper lip, which for some reason Tom thought of as touching. But why touching? Why? In a moment he felt the hardening return to him. This Aaron on the trail wasn't the Aaron he had always known, smoldering with rage, violent and reckless and unstoppable. He found himself mistrusting his son the way a sick man mistrusts a minister. Tom resolved not to make himself a burden anymore. He would say nothing, stop only if Aaron wanted to, and he'd try, he'd really, really try, to keep up the pace.

He wasn't even hungry when later they stopped for lunch, the heat having scorched the appetite right from his mouth. Though the blisters on his toes felt better, his arches pinched pain that traveled all the way to the small of his back. His neck felt swollen and bursting from the collar of his shirt, and his nose and cheeks emanated heat like tiny brick ovens. He did not complain, not even when the pinch in the soles of his feet turned into something else, more like bones shattering under heavy blows. Then his side hurt as though he'd been speared. He thought of that as he looked at the circular dwellings called the Yapashi ruins, and as he climbed down the wooden ladders that lowered into the cool, hidden dwellings, he thought of wars fought between men and of beauty turned to rubble and ruin and of the greatest tragedy of all, which is to defile God's earth with blood.

Then he was so tired he couldn't think anymore. The path ahead of him was only that particular stone, that particular dead wood that he'd have to somehow climb over. Raising his leg even only a few inches felt onerous, impossible. He'd just made it back up Alamo Canyon. He knew that because Aaron had waited for him at the mesa top to tell him they had just endured a 1,200-foot elevation change. That was just before Aaron began the descent down Capulin Canyon. Aaron had promised Capulin was the last canyon they'd cross, but Tom couldn't conceive of another step, even as his feet fell on ahead of him, somehow carrying him forward. The weather on the mesa top was breezy and almost pleasant, but on the descent, heat was contained within the crevasse and reflected from the rocky surfaces all around. The pain under his rib became something ominous, the biological knock of a death cruel enough to announce itself. He clutched at his chest and thought of heart attacks, thought of Rowan, thought of Luke and of Garret, and wished he'd have brought paper so that he could write them one last note, about how foolish he'd been to come to this desert, how foolish to leave Rowan and Luke, whom right now he missed more than even a cool shelter. His throat burned and his mouth was so dry that he dared not use it, even when Aaron, who was out of sight but still within hearing range, cast his voice across the emptiness for him. The call came again and again, a soothing wave that washed over him, causing cool shivers behind his ears.

"Dad, can you hear me? Dad, are you all right? Dad, where are you?"

Such music, Tom told himself. He thought he was beginning to lose his sanity, yet he felt like laughing, like chanting, Such music! Such music! If it was death, it was the death of a king, to lie here under the endless blanket of the sky in these ravines marked by time, and Aaron's voice filling the wind.

Then the call changed. It was no longer a wave that dispersed, a sound that skittered across the surface of the canyon, but instead it was a distinguished, narrowly pitched cry headed toward him. Aaron was climbing up the canyon walls to find him. Tom instinctively crouched behind a rock projection where scampers of shrubs cast shadows long enough to camouflage him. He thought (but perhaps he imagined it) that he saw the silhouette of Aaron wavering in the heat, his long arms loose along his body, puzzlement a sort of aura surrounding him. Like a spaceman, Tom thought to himself. He's a little spaceman in the landscape of God. He felt privileged and secretive, as though by accident he'd been blessed with the glimpse of an angel. Then the figure went away, and Tom was no longer sure of what he'd seen or why he'd hidden. He thought to use his voice now and call out for help. Aaron would find him, would help him somehow. Aaron with the duct tape to fix blisters, Aaron with tubes and filters to fix thirst. Yet Tom wouldn't call out. He'd fill his lungs to let his voice rise, and then something in his chest, like a switch, would make him stop. He'd hit on some hard kernel inside, too stubborn to knock loose. *Call out to him*, he told himself. *Call before he moves too far.*

The voice of Aaron returned to him, found him crouched behind the rocks, the bushes, but Tom wouldn't respond. Then Aaron's body met Aaron's voice again. The voice and the body came together at a fork in the path only about thirty feet away from Tom. Aaron stood with his hands on his hips, staring at the path ahead. He would turn around in the opposite direction and remain still in the sun, his fair skin red and glistening with his sweat. If Tom moved now, Aaron could see him, pick him out from the shadows and the rocks, but Tom was still. Aaron crouched down in the middle of the trail, holding his head with his hands as though it weighed more than his pack. He removed his hat and blew into it, then put it back on his head again, blowing air to the sky as if to encourage a breeze. He rubbed his face hard and long, his careful eyes studying the grade of the trail. Soon enough, Aaron would resume his ascent and find him. Perhaps sooner than that. Aaron had better than 20/10 vision, and even the slightest movement would give Tom away.

Because he remembered that, Tom was able to come out of his hiding place. Aaron saw him but didn't get up right away. The face he wore made Tom think of a statue that had been cracked on the eyeballs with a very fine scalpel. His hurt was that crack, was even the greenness of stone lime on the statue, and it was bewildered, and absolute.

Aaron said nothing as he got up. He didn't ask Tom why he was hiding, though it was clear he saw, because he'd been looking up the trail. He clapped a hand tightly around Tom's arm and squeezed for long moments, loosening his grip only to tighten it again.

At long last, he said, "I'm going ahead to the campsite, which is closer, at this point, than the Visitor's Center. I want you to wait right here. I'll come back and carry your pack for you." First he made Tom drink all that was left of the water in his bottle, then he gave Tom his own water bottle and insisted that he drink it, even though Tom didn't feel thirsty, and he knew that Aaron would need his water to get to the camp. Aaron left without his bottle anyway, taking Tom's empty plastic one and saying he had more in his pack and that he'd filter some at the campsite if necessary. Tom watched him go until Aaron took a switchback and was no longer visible, but Tom's eyes remained fixed where the last image of Aaron had been, his heart now having slowed to a reasonable pace, blood pounding steadily at his temples. It was late in the afternoon, and even the heat had began to ease, though now a suddenly cool breeze tortured the burnt skin on the back of his neck. The silence became absolute, except for the wind buffeting his ears. There were no woodpeckers, no faintly thrumming creeks, no hissing, flutelike caves, only the sounds of his own thoughts. They loosened from his head like dry leaves from a dying tree, scattering through the deep crevasse of this desert earth.

"Jesus returned from Jordan and was led by the Holy Spirit into the desert for forty days to be tempted by the devil. He ate nothing during those days and he was hungry. The devil said to him, If you are the Son of God, turn these stones into bread. And Jesus said . . ." Tom couldn't remember what Jesus said. He kicked at a pebble with his foot and thought about being hungry in the desert as impossible. The thirst would swallow everything; it would swallow even the thirst itself, so that a man would thirst for water and not know he thirsted for it. The water was too hot and inadequate and impossible. Everything was impossible. Even the landscape, with its multicolored rocks, with the agaves and cactus here, and the pine trees up above, and then ponderosa trees and grass and flowers below. Impossible. "Turn these stones into bread, and Jesus said . . . Jesus said, Man does not live by bread alone."

Tom got up and unfastened the pack from his shoulders, feeling released when it dropped with a thump to the ground. "Then the devil led Jesus to Jerusalem, made him stand on a high place and said to him, If you are the Son of God, throw yourself down, because it is written, He will command His angels to support you, lest you dash your foot against a stone. And Jesus replied, It is also written: Thou shall not put the Lord your God to the test." Tom knew there was more to that recitation, that he'd forgotten some important part of it, but something else was coming into his mind, and he couldn't stop it from encroaching on the words of the Gospel.

Then he remembered the *Take care, buddy* that Aaron had thrown back at the ranger at the Visitor's Center. He doubted instantly that Aaron would come back. What had he said in the truck in the Carson Forest about the anger he felt? Tom couldn't understand. He *didn't* understand. He didn't know his own son. He hadn't understood anything at all, hadn't seen it coming, the blisters, the bandanna, this trip, which maybe, after all, wasn't about Luke. Why should Aaron come back when he had hidden in the rocks after making Aaron climb up the face of the canyon to find him? Aaron would leave him here all night, with his water bottle and a fruit bar or two and the sleeping bag to teach him a lesson, yes, the way Tom had taught Aaron lessons when he was a boy. Because he looked like Lisette. Because he was stubborn and wouldn't obey. *It is the servant of God to inflict wrath on the evildoer . . .* Because he was proud, Tom had hidden within the rocks. Because he wouldn't admit defeat to the desert and to age.

Take care, little buddy . . .

And Luke, pleading, tugging at Rowan's robe.

Don't let him go. He's just mad at you. It's so cold.

How was he supposed to know? The way he'd cussed, banged the furniture . . . *Adolescent drama.* It was so darned cold out there. Who would have thought?

Let the cold knock some sense into the boy . . . lose his taste for bumming around.

It hadn't been Tom's intention to hurt him, but the way he'd sidled up to Luke, his tattoo still bloody under the bandages, and that silly grin on his face.

It's Frankenstein, little buddy . . . You want one too? . . . Sure, I know where you can get one just like this one . . .

Was that the way you celebrate your mother's birthday? Defiling your body with that . . . that . . . that aberration! You offend your family and God.

That bloody arm, and at thirteen already reeking of beer, his eyes bloodshot and dull. If only Aaron hadn't laughed. If only he'd just shown a little hint of fear.

Give honor where honor is due.

"Aaron," he called out, feverish, delirious. "Aaron!" He felt himself burning up, the heat he'd absorbed during the day breathing out of his skin. "Respect for your dad, Aaron. That's all I wanted to teach you. Respect." His words echoed back to him, a tinlike note to them as the sounds bounced around the bitten surface of the rock so that he thought the voice of his father had returned, speaking back to him in his own words. Tom held his face with his hands and rubbed it hard, exhaustion pressing down between his shoulder blades and on his forehead. He pressed the palms of his hands against his eyes, trying to hold back the flood of tears, but then he couldn't stop it anymore and wept, the sobs tearing out of his chest, making his body shiver. His throat ached for its dryness, but the abandonment he felt with the weeping felt deserved and even good, almost as good as the pain of his exhaustion.

He stopped weeping when he heard the voice, and when he looked down the trail again he noticed movement. He stared hard at the fork on the path, and before long he saw it was Aaron.

3

Aaron held his father up while following his own assured step across the stream they had to ford in order to get to the camp. It was almost sundown, and sheaths of angry red had begun to slide across the more complacent gray of the daylight sky. Aaron used what was left of his energies to hold his father up, weighted down by fatigue and his father's pack on his shoulders. Except for the pain of his muscles he might have thought this moment an illusion. This wasn't how he'd envisioned the culmination of this trip. What he'd wanted was a moment of perfect peace to pin the old man down with the big questions, catch him just as the old man might reach across to him with those jovial claps he liked to hand out, saying something like, Son, I'm having the best time I've ever had, for him to turn around and say, Yeah, Dad? Aren't you sorry now that you told Mom you wanted to abort me?

Not that the old man would ever admit to having fun, but at one point he thought he almost did. When they'd stopped to adjust his backpack near those tuff columns in Frijoles Canyon there had been a kind of smile on the old man's face like something close enough to what Aaron had waited for, enough to make him want to stumble in with an opening. But he'd stumbled in badly, first sarcastic, then apologetic rather than direct, and instead of the answers he sought, the regret he wanted the old man to feel, the breakdown he'd waited all his life to see, what had he managed if not his father's irritation, then his rage, then exhaustion with the strenuous pace they'd set, and finally, near hysteria? The old man was half mumbling to himself when Aaron found him sitting there, cupping his cheeks with his big hands, talking about Christ and about forgiveness and about the law of love. Exhaustion had broken him down. He looked frail, so old and beaten. Aaron felt pity for him before he could even remember how much he'd always disliked the old man. The son-of-a-bitch. The last thing Aaron wanted to feel for him was sympathy of any kind.

How many reasons did he need to hate the old bastard? If walking out on him when he was just a two year old wasn't enough, then how about his taking such good care of Garret but pretending that Aaron wasn't his responsibility at all, or being such a deadbeat as a father that Aaron had to turn to Michael Jordan for a surrogate. For god's sake, a poster! At least Michael Jordan had inspired him to play basketball, which paid off for a while during his first year in college, with a one-year scholarship. In that respect, Michael Jordan could even take credit for some of his college education, which was more than Aaron could say about his dad. That just made him sad, made him so sad to think about.

And then, of course, there was the fact that Aaron wasn't supposed to have been born at all. His father had wanted Mom to get an abortion. And maybe, who knows? Maybe Aaron was it, the breach that split them apart, a screaming little kid demanding too much attention, too much care, too much *money*.

"Your mother told you that?" Dr. Piper had asked, full of indignation. "But why?"

Well, Aaron would rather know than not know. If he was going to have to live his life without a father, then he wanted as many reasons to hate the man as he could fit in his head. And the way he was always going on and on about Aaron being a delinquent,

Aaron being the black sheep of the family, Aaron turning out wrong. Aaron had made it a point to turn out *right* just to spite him. He would make it, too, with the profession he'd gotten into. Soon enough he'd be raking in the dough, *and so there, Dad, I made it, even without your stinking money, even without your stinking love. Here I am. Kiss my sweet, rich ass.*

At the opposite bank of the stream he eased his father's pack to the ground and made him sit down. He removed his father's boots and then his own, and he replaced the dry inserts and socks that he'd taken off their feet before the fording. Even though the outer boots were wet, the dry socks and boot inserts made their feet feel comfortable.

Around them, the cottonwoods and box elders shivered as if to warn them away. The stream gurgled as it knocked over the rocks and stones in its bed, negotiating springs and gentle curves with the perpetual rearrangement of its course. The campsite was only a few miles ahead.

"You're just mildly dehydrated," he said after taking one more look at the old man's face. "We'll have to make sure you get a good rest tonight."

He looked for hints of that ghastly state his father had been in when first he'd come out from behind the rocks, farther up the canyon. He'd looked faint and sickly, and his breath was so raspy and labored that Aaron was afraid to ask him questions, afraid even the effort of an answer might kill him. He didn't look too bad, now, except for the fatigue that hung from his cheekbones and sunken eyes like a melting mask of wax. His eyes were glazed over with a faraway look. He'd lost the pointedness of his glare and even the hard set of his wide mouth, his lower lip now a little slack and chapped and ringed with dried saliva. As a kid, the face of his father had made Aaron think of the history book pictures of Roman senators, the sharp bent of that sloping forehead and his long aquiline nose adding to the authoritative demeanor he was so good at using to intimidate Aaron. It was sort of unsettling to Aaron not to see that now, even more unsettling than the obvious weakness of the old man's soft and strangely frail arms as Aaron helped him to his feet. The weight of his body when his father leaned against him wasn't nearly as imposing or even as compact as Aaron had imagined. His flesh was soft and moist with sweat, and his shirt now gave off a faintly sour odor. He wore a neglect that Aaron didn't want to see, because it made him question the strength of his own anger.

With the backpack strapped on him and his father sometimes leaning on his shoulder, the two miles to the camp felt treacherous and long. At the campsite, his father wanted to be helpful, suddenly peppy in his tone of voice but slack in his posture, limp arms hanging from his slumping shoulders. Aaron hurriedly pitched camp. He was too tired to cook a hot meal, so he handed his father a few beef jerkies, trail mix, and a granola bar. Then he tied the food pack inside a plastic bag and with a rope hung it up a tree some fifty feet away from their tent so that predators wouldn't come too near if the smell of food attracted them. He and his father ate the food silently and drank the water they had left, which wasn't as much as he had hoped. Aaron had tried to filter more water at the stream, but the clay had clogged the filter so badly that it had become unusable. Aaron thought about trying to clean it with a toothbrush, but he'd need fresh water for that, and the method was not always effective. Besides, he was too tired.

As he chewed his food he looked up at the sky, which seemed unusually bright for the time of day, glowing with a subdued, purplish light. The basin of the canyon was lush by comparison to the mesa, but still it was dressed with an eerie kind of flora, so different from the noisy, bristling palm trees and the loud-colored tropical flowers that adorned the gardens, the backyards, the street medians of South Florida. He'd been backpacking far from home before, but he'd never been to New Mexico, and he found the brusque changes of its landscape surprising and pleasingly alien.

After some time in silence, Aaron looked over at his father, who still seemed somewhat dazed, if calm. He still wore the large straw hat he'd bought at the airport in Albuquerque and under it the bandanna that Aaron had lent him.

"You can take off your hat now," he told his father. Anger burned up his chest as he spoke. The exquisite delicateness of the moment when he'd wet the bandanna in the creek, that had seemed then almost too tender for Aaron to indulge, made him furious now. *Like a servant, on my knees, tending to his wounds.*

Master, would you like your feet washed with my ointments?
"You could say thank you, you know?"

His father glimpsed at him from under the rim of his straw hat. Though his skin had returned to its usual yellowish tan, it still retained an oily kind of wariness. The eyes brimmed with a wet annoyance as his arm jerkily removed his hat and beat it on the ground beside him. Finally, his mouth had set into its usual sternness.

"You could show a little gratitude," Aaron said. He felt the tone of his voice rising, but instead of taking a warning from it, he became even more irritated. "Why didn't you tell me that you were getting tired? Why didn't you ask me to stop? Why didn't you drink your water when you felt it getting so hot?"

His father clasped his hands around his knees and grinned at Aaron as if amused.

"God delivered all to disobedience, that He might have mercy upon all."

Aaron didn't think it was funny. He stood up and kicked dust on his father's boots. "Are you preaching at me? Do you want to talk Bible now? How come you get to feel so righteous about yourself after what you'd done to my mother. No, forget that. Let's talk about what you've done to me. Me. Me. Aaron." He pounded his chest, as though his father needed directions to see him. "You remember, Dad, when I asked you for money for college? I had a basketball scholarship, and all I wanted, *all I needed*, was a loan, for my books, for a car. Not very much to ask, was it? But you, you gave everything to Garret, new car, new books, full tuition paid at a private school, and for Luke you'd sell your teeth if you had to. But what about me, huh, Dad? What did I get when I asked you for help? Do you remember what you said, Dad, the only time I've *ever* asked you for help?"

The skin around the old man's eyes had bunched up tightly so that long, deep crinkles formed over his cheekbones.

"No one who lights a lamp conceals it with a vessel or sets it under a bed; rather, he places it on a lamp stand so that those who enter may see the light."

"Wrong!" Aaron shouted. "You said, I have my son to think about. *My son.* And what am I, exactly? What am *I*?"

"For there is nothing hidden that will not become visible, and nothing secret that will not be known and come to light."

"What? What're you talking about?"

"Take care, then, how you hear. To anyone who has, more will be given, and from the one who has not, even what he seems to have will be taken away." Aaron's father looked up at Aaron with his mouth closed, breathing through his nose. In the dusk and with the pale glow of their camping lantern, his father's eyes seemed to shimmer. The grooves around his mouth and nose were deep, and jowls of fat hung timidly from his jaw.

Aaron stood up, his hands bunching into fists. He glowered at his father and was outraged and wanted so badly to feel angry enough to strike at him, to hit him in the mouth, to release somehow the betrayal he had carried on him these twenty-something years. But the more he looked at his father, the more the anger ebbed away, giving place instead to an irksome kind of pity.

His father laced his hands around his knees, his mouth a dried, frowning groove. His eyes tried to follow something on the ground, the path of an ant or something imaginary, then returned to fix on Aaron.

"Of course you've got nothing but Godspeak for me," Aaron said. "What else could you possibly say? And what the hell does God have to do with me anyway?" he raged suddenly, his voice booming across the immense basin of the canyon. "How come He wasn't around when you left us all behind like a sack of shit."

"God is everywhere. He is everything," his father said. He spoke quietly into his own chest, as if himself uncertain of the truth of his own words. Then he looked up, his wide eyes wet and smoky. "You were a punk," he shook a finger at Aaron, his voice struggling to rise, its intended power choking in his throat. He pushed a hand to the ground and tried to get up, but when Aaron stepped toward him, responding to the challenge, he seemed to think better of it, and he sat back down. "You were a drunk. At thirteen!"

Aaron breathed, his chest swelling.

His father looked farther off, where a whiff of wind had set off a rustling in the shrubs. "I sent money," he repeated, his head nervously returning to stalk Aaron, like a bird sensing prey. "You, a little punk," he muttered, a popping log in a dying fire.

"And Garret . . . I tried to make him a man, but he ̄ . . . he was broken . . . I had Luke. I had Rowan. You were a drunk. At thirteen! With your tattoos. I had Luke! I tried with Garret, but he was broken. A man can only put his faith in God. A man can only let God judge him. How would I know you would go out in the snow? At thirteen, you drank! Rowan knew it. She warned me . . ." he babbled on.

Aaron held his breath. Once, twice, he feinted toward the old man, wanting to lift him by his shirt, shake him like a rag doll, push him off into some shrubs and beat him and leave him there to rot in this desert, with his babble and his bitterness and his blind and obtuse faith. But every time he leapt for him his anger failed him, subsiding just as it should be rising, inexplicably abated by the sorry posture of the old man. This stooped stick figure before him, so frail he seemed a stranger: he made no sense, not the way he looked or the things he said.

This was certainly not the man who'd picked him up with such ease years ago, thrown him against the balustrade of that stairwell, nor was he the man whose hands seemed so large Aaron watched them as they lifted and gestured and moved across the air at the dinner table, so graceful in spite of their size that they emulated the sleight of hand of a prestidigitator. He wasn't even the man he was only yesterday, reading the Bible in the window booth of a family restaurant while Aaron stood across the street leaning against a parking meter, a hand on his chest as if to prevent his hurt from spilling on the sidewalk. In this desert, something had happened to this man. He was like a tree that had been suffocated by the hot smoke of a fire. The shape of him was still there, rooted in its space as usual, but the verve had somehow been spirited out of him. He was, finally, only an old man. And by contrast he was himself, finally, just an angry young man futilely kicking dust on an old man's boots.

"Fuck you, Dad," he said, waving him away with a gesture. He spat on the ground and ambled off, the old man's rabid babble dispersing with the sound of his boots. He grinned at the sky and saw that the moon had began to appear on the wildly streaked sky above them. She was red, bloodshot like a drunken eye. It made him think of an Italian proverb Mom had once repeated to him, something about red moons. (She had spent a summer in Florence studying Renaissance architecture.) "*Luna rossa, o piscia, o sof-fia,*" she chirped. "A red moon—she will make the night either piss or blow." Aaron remembered it, because he'd been struck by the notion of a moon being a she, and now the moon made him think of Mom.

When later he settled into his sleeping bag next to his father, who was still muttering words about God, he thought of her again. He closed his eyes and tried to imagine what she would say if he'd ever tell her about this night. I failed you, he told her in his head. He knew Dr. Piper wouldn't like that. He was supposed to take responsibility for his own feelings. He wasn't battling his mother's battles; he was here for himself. He shifted inside the sleeping bag, trying to push the thought away, but Mom was there now, critical and strangely sympathetic; she was before him, her voice that soothing whisper suggesting her earthy sensibility. He fell asleep with her round, bony face set firmly in front of him, pale and yellowish and permanent like the familiar yet always unknowable moon.

He woke up to the noise of wind boxing the walls of the tent, and, startled, he sat up, unzipping himself from his sleeping bag. The howl of the wind and the flapping of the tent and fly frightened him. Aaron looked over at his father, and when his eyes adjusted to the darkness he realized his father was awake, the whites of his eyes glowing strangely in the dark.

"Don't worry," he reassured him. "It's all right, nothing to get worked up about." He was responsible for this, his stupid idea, backpacking with an older man who'd not exerted his body like this in years. How foolish could he be? He'd said not to worry, but the hissing and the flapping felt harder than any storm Aaron had ever been caught in, and he was worried that a seam might rip. "Go back to sleep," he told his father. "We're perfectly safe." He moved his and his father's packs away from the tent walls and lay back down, turning his back on his father in his sleeping bag, wanting his father to believe there really was nothing to worry about. Moisture had already formed at the seams and the corners of the tent, and a short time later water began to seep in at the edges from the ground. Aaron scooted gently toward the center of the tent, content that there was still plenty of space for them to stay dry. He doubted that he could fall back asleep, especially when lightning and thunder seemed to crack closer and harder each time. He'd keep an eye on the floor and make sure he'd do what he could to keep them both dry. He'd read that in New Mexico it rarely rained. He seemed to remember eighteen inches a year average precipitation, but then he also remembered that flash floods and hard storms were not an unusual occurrence in the summer. Still, it was easier to blame it on his bad luck, the rotten way everything had turned out, starting with the fire in the Carson forest.

With each flash of lightning, the tent walls became veined with flickering shadows. The earth seemed to explode around them with the boom of thunder. Then the wind seemed to rise, a howl to accompany the violent beating of the mesh and fabric, the trees bristling and hissing with thrashing limbs. The howl reminded Aaron of the noise he'd heard all night, years ago, when hurricane Andrew had passed over Florida. He'd stayed crouched in the tub of a windowless bathroom with Garret and Mom, hearing that same, incessant howl hour after hour and the thumping and banging and crashing of things outside. When they'd come out in the morning, the house in which they'd lived had collapsed around them. There was no roof, no side walls, nothing but rubble and mud. The howl of this wind was similar, sometimes high-pitched and then something like a wail or a low moan. Aaron felt his skin become electric with his fear. The skeleton of the tent was rattling under the pressure, the poles of the tent making strange cracking sounds. Aaron sat up, and in that very instant the pole at his side, the wind side, bowed in. Unbelieving, Aaron lifted his hand to push the pole back to its outward curve. He started to hyperventilate, suddenly uncertain about the safety of his shelter.

His father sat up with a slow, groggy kind of movement. "Anything I can do?"

"No, Dad, don't worry. It's normal, it happens all the time," he lied. "You need to get your rest. Get some sleep."

"You sure?"

"Yeah. It's going to be all right."

Aaron's father lay back down, and, after a moment or so, his breathing regained the heavy steadiness it had before with the rhythms of sleep. Aaron wondered why the ranger hadn't warned them about the oncoming storm. When the violent gust that had attacked the tent seemed to relent, Aaron hesitantly let go of the pole. He worried most of all that the seams would rip, exposing them to the weather. He thought he'd want to kill the ranger, at least report him, but then he realized that perhaps the ranger hadn't known about the storm. It had been early in the day when they'd seen him. Aaron looked at his watch and saw that it was almost four in the morning. It was conceivable that the storm had been unexpected.

He wanted to lie back down, as he felt wearied from the hike, but he didn't dare. The wind had only temporarily abated, and suddenly it had gained its strength again, the haunting moan returning, revisiting his adolescent terrors. He burned to know the limitations of his shelter, even though knowing at this point would do him little good. He remained sitting up, his eyes fixed on the pole that had given earlier, his eyes peeled in the darkness for any hints of breaches in the fabric. The wind became a furious boxer, fighting with relentless fervor the mesh on the little dome, the poles straining under its bewildering strength. For as long as the fly held staked to the ground, Aaron knew the tent would remain relatively dry. He hoped the wind wouldn't rip a loop from its stake, or tear the fabric, or strip the entire fly from over the tent. If the fly failed, there would be no way to keep dry. Then lightning flashed like an X-ray, brightening the dome. Aaron saw his own shadow move with clipped and jerky movements. Because the water had begun to advance, seeping in from the corners, Aaron bent down over his sleeping father to pull his pack still farther away from the tent walls. He'd not seen the object coming, except as a quick, bloating shadow zipping over the strained curve of the tent dome. The noise had been hollow and sharp at first, then metallic and confused. Something snapped, then something brushed against him, announcing itself with a fine, faint scratching of his arm. The tent deflated on one side, the moist fabric shrouding him as, baffled, he sat up. The tent remained relatively normal above his father, as if held up by a giant air bubble but having lost most of its original domelike shape. Aaron quickly groped the wet tent fabric that had fallen over him, feeling for the poles, trying to understand what had happened. At first he'd thought one of the poles had bowed in so far that it had broken, but when a clump of tiny objects scratched against the tarp (thin sticks and leaves, Aaron guessed), he realized that a tree branch or other flying debris had knocked down the poles.

"Dad?" he whispered. There was no reply. His father's body had probably suffered more abuse than it ought to have, and the man had surrendered completely to his need for rest. Soon, however, he would wake up, as the rain would certainly start to seep in due to the weakened tension of the fabric. Aaron moved quickly, searching in the darkness under the sagging wet tarp for his pack, hoping to find his shell, boots, and flashlight. If the pole wasn't broken, then the debris had somehow dislodged one or both of the poles from their pins, and all he needed to do was to reinsert them.

"Aaron," his father moaned.

"Don't worry, Dad, I'll fix it."

"I'll help?" Aaron's father's voice was heavy and drenched with sleep. Aaron sat back on his haunches, inexplicably overwhelmed.

"No," he faltered, the weight of the responsibility he felt cutting his breath, "no, you wouldn't know what to do. I'll take care of it. Stay calm, and try to sleep."

Outside the night pissed rain on him exactly the way the Italian proverb said. Rivulets streamed down his face and on his back under the collar of his shell. He pointed his flashlight over the wet, lumpy clump of fabric that was his side of the tent, the wind blowing at him so hard he had to lean into it just to steady himself in his space. The flashlight illuminated little beyond the tiny lances of water that pelted his mouth and eyes so hard they hurt him. He crouched and braced himself against the inconceivable wind, which robbed him of his breath and tried to steal the flashlight from his stubborn grip. The fly had remained staked steadily to the ground, but, having lost the tension of the tent dome, it flapped and billowed and whipped its loose body obscenely, breaking its arch only to lash against the weakened bubble of the tent below. Aaron fumbled under the whipping tarp, his hands searching frantically for the ring and pin, those nylon loops in which the poles needed to be fitted in order to preserve the proper degree of curvature. He lodged his flashlight between his knees, afraid the wind would rip it from him and leave him fumbling in the dark. He cried and howled against the wind that so abused him, determined not to be defeated by it, his voice overcome by the constant cracking and rumbling of thunder. His fingers slipped. The nylon rings had swollen in the humidity. The tent was a live animal unwilling to be subdued, its slippery body breathing and writhing to the beat of the storm's chaotic rush. It seemed to him he'd been out there for hours already, the mud conspiring with the streaming water and the bullying wind to make his task impossible. He would force the pole into place, then feel it slip between his hands from the muddied ring, the fabric misbehaving from the deep rise in humidity and the sudden drop of temperature that the storm had brought. He'd try again and again to secure the pole into its pin, his grunting and moaning pushing from his plexus with the effort. Finally, he succeeded, the tips of his fingers burning with the pressure he'd applied. He moved on his hands and knees around the tent for the other pole, but instantly, as he cast the tenuous spar of his flashlight toward the flapping tarp, he saw by the sharp point pushing against the fly that the second pole had been split, broken in its sleeve, either by the wind or by the debris that had hit the tent earlier. Had it been a clear night or had the wind been even only a little less fierce, Aaron might have tried to secure the breakage with duct tape, perhaps guying the tent to strengthen tension. But he knew there was no way he would be able to do so now in this weather, with this darkness, with the rain something painful on his skin. All he could do was crawl back to the tent's entrance, his hands muddy, his fingers stinging with cuts and scratches, and his face buffeted and punished by the curse of this improbable night. The tent stood at an odd, billowy angle, leaning on its shattered pole, the dented arch of its shell as sad a sight as he knew himself to be.

He took that image with him inside and held it under his eyelids as he removed his wet garments in the vestibule, attempting to disrupt as little as possible the frail, wind-buffeted structure of the tent. He held up the pole where it had broken, no longer hopeful that he could maintain the integrity, wanting only to keep the water from collecting into pockets on the ceiling, wanting to keep his father dry and undisturbed through his badly needed rest. He looked at the slumped, limp shape of his father in the dark and felt his lips begin to tremble and his chest fill with an odd tremor. He heard the laughter push out of his throat even before he understood that he was laughing and why. But then the laughter washed over him like a wave, hilarity trickling in rivulets through the length of his tendons and muscles. Tears clung to his eyelashes as he laughed, filled with the comic absurdity of his predicament. Here he was, holding up the ceiling of a sagging, wet, flapping tent in the middle of a rainstorm in the desert with his father whom he had not ever really known and who slept now, slept calmly and deeply, oblivious to the rain and to the storm and to the flimsy tent that sheltered him or even to the son who held it up for him so he could rest.

The Iowa Short Fiction Award and John Simmons Short Fiction Award Winners

2002
Her Kind of Want,
Jennifer S. Davis
The Kind of Things Saints Do,
Laura Valeri

2001
Ticket to Minto: Stories of India and America,
Sohrab Homi Fracis
Fire Road, Donald Anderson

2000
Articles of Faith, Elizabeth Oness
Troublemakers, John McNally

1999
House Fires, Nancy Reisman
Out of the Girls' Room and into the Night,
Thisbe Nissen

1998
Friendly Fire, Kathryn Chetkovich
The River of Lost Voices: Stories from Guatemala,
Mark Brazaitis

1997
Thank You for Being Concerned and Sensitive,
Jim Henry
Within the Lighted City,
Lisa Lenzo

1996
Hints of His Mortality,
David Borofka
Western Electric,
Don Zancanella

1995
Listening to Mozart,
Charles Wyatt
May You Live in Interesting Times,
Tereze Glück

1994
The Good Doctor,
Susan Onthank Mates
Igloo among Palms,
Rod Val Moore

1993
Happiness,
Ann Harleman
Macauley's Thumb,
Lex Williford
Where Love Leaves Us,
Renée Manfredi

1992
My Body to You,
Elizabeth Searle
Imaginary Men,
Enid Shomer

1991
The Ant Generator,
Elizabeth Harris
Traps,
Sondra Spatt Olsen

1990
A Hole in the Language,
Marly Swick

Erica Bleeg

Laura Valeri received her MFA from the
University of Iowa Writers' Workshop. Her
stories have been published in *Gulf Stream
Magazine* and the *Ruben's Quarterly Review*. She currently lives in south Florida.